HIGH STAKES BRIDE

MARGERY SCOTT

CLOVER RIDGE PRESS

HIGH STAKES BRIDE

ROMANTIC SUSPENSE

A Time for Secrets
No One to Tell
The Stranger She Knows
A Question of Guilt

HIGH STAKES BRIDE

CHAPTER 1

"Where are you going, Pa?" Chloe Taggart wiped her hands on a towel as she stood in the doorway between the kitchen and the dining room of Millie's Diner.

Elvin Taggart plucked his jacket off the hook on the wall. "I won't be long, poppet," he said. "Just meeting up with some folks. I'll be back before you know it."

She wished he would stop using the nickname he'd given her when she was a little girl. After all, she was a full-grown woman now that she'd had her nineteenth birthday three weeks ago. "It's late," she protested.

"I know what time it is." He closed the gap between them, cupped her face between his giant hands and planted a kiss on her forehead. "Be a good girl and finish the dishes while I'm gone, otherwise we'll have it all to do in the morning before we open."

He brushed against her as he passed by and then strode through the dining room to the outside door. The bell jangled when he tugged the door open and went out, pulling it shut behind him.

Chloe let out a sigh. She was tired, and all she wanted to do was go upstairs to their small apartment and crawl into bed. But if she did, her father wouldn't leave the dishes until morning. He'd do them himself when he got back from wherever he'd gone. She only hoped he hadn't gone to the saloon.

No, she assured herself, he wouldn't go there. He'd promised after the last time.

Only a few more months, she reminded herself as she lifted the pot of boiling water off the stove and poured it into the cold water already in the washbasin on the worktable. With her wages her father paid her, she'd have enough money by spring to leave Rocky Ridge. She'd go to New York City, or to California. Maybe even to Europe. She was a good cook. She could find work in one of the fancy restaurants in the cities while she saw the world.

She'd be free—free to live her life the way she saw fit, without anyone controlling her every movement. No one to tell her when to eat, when to sleep, where she could go.

Fantasies of the adventures she'd have filled her mind as she scrubbed and dried the stacks of plates and mugs and set them on the shelf ready for the next day.

She'd miss her father. She knew that. And he'd

miss her. After all, it had just been the two of them since she was six years old. But life was waiting for her outside of Rocky Ridge, and it couldn't come soon enough.

The tinkle of the piano keys in the corner of The Black Bear Saloon died out. Voices faded. Silence fell over the smoke-filled room.

In the center of the crowded saloon, two men faced each other across a scarred wooden table. Five men had started the poker game hours before, but now only Elvin Taggart and Austin Hayward were left.

Elvin lifted the glass of whiskey to his lips and drained it, then raised his hand. "Horace," he called out to the bartender. "Another one."

Austin laid his cards face down on the table. "Don't you think you've had enough, Elvin?"

Austin knew Elvin wasn't usually much of a drinker, but he did have a problem staying away from a poker game. Austin had tried to refuse him when he'd approached the table earlier, but the man had been dead set on joining in.

Horace brought the bottle of whiskey to the table and filled Elvin's glass. Elvin took a drink and set it down beside him.

"Well, Elvin?" Austin rested his elbows on the table and mentally counted the coins on the table in front of his opponent. Elvin had enough money to match Austin's bet, but not to raise it. "What are you doing? Calling or folding?"

Austin didn't want to be the one who wiped Elvin out, but he was the only player left. For a few moments, he considered folding himself. He could afford to lose the money. Elvin couldn't.

The problem with that was that Elvin would realize no decent poker player—which Austin was—would fold with the cards he had. He'd figure out pretty quickly what Austin was up to, and he'd be angry, maybe even angry enough to start some real trouble.

No, Austin had to see it through, even though he was pretty sure Elvin was going to lose.

And even more on Austin's mind was the fact that if Elvin lost, so would Chloe. And that bothered him more than anything.

Anything that affected Chloe Taggart affected him. She'd affected him since the day she started school right after her family moved to Rocky Ridge. That morning, Toby Winfield had dunked her pigtails in the inkwell. She hadn't said a word, had just turned around and punched him in the nose. She'd spent the rest of the day in the corner as punishment, but Toby had never bothered her again.

Austin was pretty sure he started falling in love with Chloe that day, and he'd completely fallen in love with her the one time she danced with him at the Fourth of July dance five years ago.

He was well aware of how people thought of him - that these days, he was considered the most eligible bachelor in Rocky Ridge. Mothers paraded their unmarried daughters in front of him regularly, hoping he'd marry one of them, but none of them could hold a candle to Chloe.

Too bad Chloe didn't feel the same way about him. She'd never thought of him as anything more than a friend, and he'd never had the nerve to let her know how he felt about her.

Dragging his mind back to the game, he sat quietly, hoping Elvin would realize he was in too deep and fold his hand.

No such luck!

Elvin scrubbed the whiskers on his chin and studied his cards. He gathered the bills and coins in front of him and shoved them all into the pile in the center of the table. "I'll see your hundred and raise you …" He reached into his pocket, his face reddening when he came up empty-handed.

"Elvin, you're out."

"No!" He turned to the tall, barrel-chested man drying a glass behind the bar. "Horace, lend me a hunnerd, will ya? You know I'm good for it."

The bartender put the glass on a shelf behind the bar before he answered. "Sorry, Elvin, I can't do it."

Elvin turned his attention to the men sitting on the sidelines. "Evan? Mitch …?"

Austin watched as the crowd began to turn away

from the game. It was obvious they didn't want to get dragged into Elvin's plea for money.

"Elvin, just fold and we'll get this over with," Austin said.

Elvin's eyes narrowed. "No. I got somethin' even better'n money."

Austin was curious now. "What's that?"

"Millie's."

"The diner?" Austin couldn't believe Elvin would risk his livelihood. Elvin had owned the diner at the other end of town as far back as he could remember. It was named after Chloe's mother, who'd passed shortly after it opened. "Are you crazy?"

"Nope." Elvin downed the rest of the whiskey and slammed the glass on the table. "Well?"

"Elvin, I think you're making a big mistake," Austin said. "You've had a lot to drink, and—"

"I know what I'm doin', Austin. Now, you gonna bet or fold?"

"Elvin, it's your living—"

Elvin leaned forward, resting his elbows on the table. "Bet or fold," Elvin repeated.

Whether it was the whiskey or the fact that he'd suddenly realized how close he was to going home with empty pockets, the almost threatening tone of Elvin's voice surprised Austin. Elvin wasn't known to have a temper, but his face was flushed, and he was holding his cards so tight his knuckles were white.

Austin saw the tension in Elvin's jaw, heard the

short shallow breaths. He couldn't fold. Elvin would demand to see his cards. He always did.

"I'll match you," Austin said. "How much do you think the diner is worth?"

Elvin gave him a number.

It was less than Austin expected, but still a tidy sum of money. He reached into his pocket and took out his leather pocketbook. Withdrawing a wad of bills, he counted them out and slid them into the center of the table. "Call."

Elvin slowly chose a card and laid it face up on the table, as if he was savoring the victory he was convinced was only moments away.

"Ten," he said. Then, plucking another card out of his hand, he put it beside the first one. "Queen."

Austin frowned. What kind of hand did he have? A straight? Two pairs?

The third card was a ten. The fourth was another ten.

There wasn't a sound in the saloon. It was as if everyone in the place had even stopped breathing.

With a grin, Elvin carefully placed the last card beside the others and slapped his hand down on top of them all. "Ten," he said smugly. "Four tens."

Austin looked down at his own cards. There was no way out now.

"Well?" Elvin's voice broke into his thoughts. "Lessee what you got."

Austin dropped his cards on the table. Five cards.

One color. From four to eight. A gasp rose up, filling the silence.

Elvin's face flushed. "How … you cheated … you musta cheated …"

"I'm sorry, Elvin," Austin said quietly, "but you know me well. You know I don't cheat. Look, we can just forget this—"

Elvin's chair scraped against the floor as he bounded to his feet. "Won't forget … I pay my debts. Let's go. I'll get you the deed right now."

"There's no rush—"

"Need to get it over with. Unnerstand?"

Austin nodded, got to his feet and followed Elvin out of the saloon into the night.

Chloe woke from an exhausted sleep to the sound of her father's voice coming from the diner downstairs. It was louder than usual and he was slurring his words. She sighed. He'd been drinking, which meant she'd likely have to get up and make coffee for him. Hopefully he wasn't so drunk she'd have to put him to bed.

But why was he talking to himself? And what was he rambling about? She couldn't quite make out the words, but he was saying something about the diner … and debts …

She crawled out of bed and shoved her arms into her robe, then opened her bedroom door just as another voice interrupted him. A very familiar voice.

Austin Hayward.

What in Heaven's name was her father doing, inviting Austin home at this time of night?

It was highly improper for her to be seen in a robe by anyone other than her family, but right now, she didn't care. Hurrying down the stairs, she stopped dead when she came upon the two men in the kitchen.

Her father was leaning against the wall, looking like he was about to crumple onto the floor. He lifted his head as she entered and looked at her, his eyes rheumy. Were those … tears … in his eyes?

Austin stood beside him, his arms outstretched, ready to catch him if he fell. Then he gently urged him toward a chair and supported him until he sat down at the table.

"I'm sorry, poppet," her father muttered.

Sorry? Sorry for what? A sense of dread washed over her. Something was very wrong. She cast a questioning glance at Austin, trying not to notice the sympathetic look in his eyes or the way he seemed to be avoiding her gaze.

There was only one possible explanation for why Austin had brought her father home. He'd been gambling again, and the sooner she found out the extent of his loss, the sooner she could figure out how to recover from it. She turned her attention to her father, his head bowed. "How much did you lose this time, Papa?"

"I was so sure..."

"I tried to stop him, Chloe," Austin put in.

Elvin looked up, meeting Austin's gaze. "That you did, son."

"How much?" Chloe couldn't keep the irritation out of her voice.

"It's not how much," Austin said. "It's what."

Chloe didn't understand. "What are you talking about?"

Austin's voice softened. "I'm sorry, Chloe. He wagered the diner."

Chloe stood for a moment, unable to even take a breath. The room spun, and she gripped the back of the chair for support. She couldn't have heard him right? Her father gambled—a lot! He lost a lot of money, and every time, he'd apologize and promise it wouldn't happen again.

But to risk the diner ...

"He wouldn't ..." Even as the words left her mouth, she knew they were only wishes, that Austin wouldn't lie to her.

Swallowing past the lump that had formed in her throat, she croaked out the uppermost question in her mind. "Who did he lose it to?"

He hesitated for a moment before he answered. Finally, he spoke quietly. "Me."

"You!" she spat out. "How could you do this to him ... to us?"

"Not his ... fault ..." Elvin's speech was almost impossible to understand now, his eyes closing. A moment later, his head dropped to the table and he fell asleep.

Chloe rose to her full height, took in a few deep breaths to calm her racing heart and the anger that felt as though she was suffocating in it, and met his gaze. "Please leave now," she ground out. "I'll have the deed sent out to your ranch in the morning."

"Let me help you—"

"I don't need your help," she countered, unable to keep the bitterness out of her voice. He'd taken advantage of her father, and she wanted nothing to do with him. "I'll deal with him myself. Now just go."

Austin looked as if he was going to refuse. Then he shrugged. "If you change your mind, you know where I am."

Yes, she knew where he was—at the Bar-W, his family's fancy ranch outside of town.

She turned away from him, waiting until the door closed behind him before she slumped into the other vacant chair and let her tears fall.

Her father had really done it this time. What was it about a deck of cards that had such a hold on him? What was it about them that made him - a kind and thoughtful man and loving father - forget about all his responsibilities and think only of winning a game of chance?

He'd risked everything they owned. And he'd lost. What were they going to do now?

CHAPTER 2

Austin rammed the pitchfork into the pile of straw on the barn floor and heaved it into the empty stall. Sweat trickled down his face, and his shirt clung to his chest. He paused, took off his hat and wiped his brow with his shirt sleeve.

He'd been working since just after dawn, doing his best to put the events of the night before out of his mind. Trying, and failing.

No matter how much he pushed himself, worked his muscles until they burned, he couldn't get rid of the vision of Chloe's face when he'd told her about what had happened, and the part he'd played in it.

He hated to see her unhappy, and if she'd let him, he'd do his best to make sure she never had an unhappy minute for the rest of her life.

She'd come into the kitchen, her eyes heavy with fatigue, stray curls from her dark brown braid framing her creamy skin. She'd been surprised to see him there. He didn't usually spend time with her father. And when he'd told her he was the one her father had lost the diner to, she'd been devastated. Hell, he might as well have told her somebody died.

She hated him now. He'd known Chloe for years, and they'd always been friends. Well, if he was being completely honest, their friendship had been on shaky ground a couple times—the day he'd laughed at her when she'd fallen into the mud puddle, for one. Oh, and the time he'd tossed her in the river one summer afternoon when Bobby Denholm had dared him to.

Other than those two incidents and a few minor disagreements over the years, they'd been good friends. Well, they had been until she'd started growing up.

He had no idea what had happened to cause it, but something had seemed to change, to shift. On the surface, they were still friendly, but their relationship was different.

Now it looked like she'd hate him forever. She hadn't even given him a chance to explain that he'd tried to stop her father from betting the diner on that hand of cards.

His brother, Jamie, ambled into the barn. "You almost done?" he asked. "I could use an extra pair of hands fixing that leak in the bunkhouse roof. The boys are all out riding the fence lines. That storm the other night knocked down one of them in the north pasture. Thought it would be a good idea to check the others before we lose the cattle."

"Just about done," Austin replied.

"Ma told me what happened last night," Jamie said. "We all know how much you like to eat, but the only thing you know about cooking is how to eat somebody else's. What are you going to do with a diner?"

Austin shrugged as he picked up a shovel and began scooping the used straw and waste into a wheelbarrow standing nearby. "Nothing. I don't want it."

"Are you going to give it back to Elvin?"

Austin shook his head. "I tried to do just that last night, but he wouldn't hear of it. Of course, he was drunk so maybe this morning, he'll think better of turning down my offer. Somehow I doubt it, though. Elvin Taggart is one mule-headed old man."

"So, what are you going to do with it? Leave it empty?"

"I'm not sure. I do have an idea, though. And if it works out the way I hope it will, everybody will be happy."

Jamie frowned. "What are you up to?"

Austin had lain awake the whole night trying to come up with a solution. At some point just before dawn, at that moment just before exhausted sleep claimed him, a plan formed in his brain - a plan that not only would give Elvin back his diner, but would give Austin the one thing in the world he wanted most.

There was only one major obstacle – Chloe.

Somehow, he'd have to convince Chloe to go along with it. "You'll find out soon enough," Austin said with a grin. "Now, if you're not going to help, get out of here and leave me alone so I can get finished. Then I can give you a hand with the roof."

Jamie didn't need to be told twice. As soon as he was gone, Austin went back to work. If he could get through his chores quick enough and the leak in the bunkhouse roof wasn't too bad, he'd take a ride into town and make Chloe an offer she wouldn't be able to refuse.

He was shoveling straw from the last stall into the wheelbarrow when he heard the sound of hoofbeats and the creaking and rumbling of a wagon or buckboard in the yard. It was early for visitors, but when the sound stopped right in front of the barn instead of passing by and going toward the house, he leaned the shovel against the gate to the stall and brushed a few pieces of straw off his pants.

He took a step toward the barn door at the same time as a woman appeared in the entrance, silhouetted against the late morning sun. He squinted, recognizing Chloe's curves. He'd memorized every inch of her years ago, and when he closed his eyes at night, his mind returned to the one time he'd held her in his arms. He could still feel her body pressed against his, her lavender scent filling his nostrils, her silky curls brushing against his cheek.

The Founder's Day dance. The night had been warm, the sky clear with a million stars overhead.

Lanterns hanging on the posts lining the street had cast shadows on the makeshift dance floor.

They'd been doing a quadrille, and somehow, she'd tripped over something. He'd reached out to stop her from falling and she'd landed in his arms. She'd snaked her arms around his neck, her breath tickling his neck.

Their eyes had met, and time had stood still, but all too soon, she'd pulled away.

Now, as her slim hips swayed with each step as she walked toward him, his insides lurched and lust spiked him low in his belly.

"Morning, Chloe." He smiled, but even though he couldn't see the details of her face, he knew she wouldn't be returning it.

The light dimmed behind her as she came into the barn and stopped in front of him. She eyed him steadily, but it was plain to see on her face that she hadn't slept well.

"How's your father this morning?" Austin asked. "I suspect he's a bit under the weather after all the whiskey he put away last night."

"He was still asleep when I left," she answered.

"I was going to come see you this afternoon as soon as I got my chores finished and I cleaned myself up a bit."

"Why?" Her voice was bitter. "In a hurry to get your hands on the deed to the diner? I told you I'd bring it out here this morning."

He let out a breath. He understood why she was

angry. If the tables were turned, he'd be madder than a hornet, too. Anybody came along and threatened the Bar-W and they'd have to take it from his cold, dead hands.

"No," he replied. "I wanted to talk to you—"

"There's nothing to talk about." She dug into her reticule and pulled out a folded piece of paper. It was yellowed with age, and something had splattered it at one time, leaving dark stains. "Here's the deed," she said, her voice breaking. "I've already started packing, and we'll be gone by the end of the week."

"Chloe," he began, but she'd already turned away and was marching out of the barn. "Wait!"

For a moment, he didn't think she'd heard him, but then she stopped. She didn't turn around immediately, but after another second or two, she squared her shoulders and turned to face him.

He closed the gap between them, the deed still in his hand.

"What is it, Austin?" she snapped. "I have a lot to do."

He'd spent hours trying to find the right words to explain his plan in such a way that Chloe wouldn't either laugh at him or slap his face. When dawn broke that morning, he still hadn't found them. Now he had no choice but to blurt it out the best way he knew how.

"Please don't hate me," he said.

His plea seemed to take some of the wind out of her sails. "I don't hate you," she replied, resignation

26

taking the place of the bitterness he'd heard only moments before.

"We used to be friends," he reminded her.

"That's true, but we were children then. Things change."

"They don't have to," he pointed out. "I didn't change."

"Really?" She studied him, her gaze sliding from his head to his feet. "Then how do you explain that you're not the scrawny boy with the mop of shaggy blond hair that taught me how to catch minnows in a jar now?"

"Maybe I've changed on the outside, but on the inside, I'm still the same." That wasn't exactly true. He'd matured, he'd figured out how he wanted to spend his life and who he wanted to spend it with. "Did I hurt you somehow that I don't know about? Did I insult you or treat you badly?"

She shook her head. "No," she said, her voice little more than a whisper. "You've always treated me with kindness and respect."

"Then what happened?"

She didn't answer. "You have the deed. Now I have to go."

"Chloe," he said softly. "I don't want to take this."

"You won it fair and square." She blinked, and Austin saw the effort she was making not to cry.

"That may be so, but I don't want it. I don't know anything about running a diner. I can barely boil water without burning the pot dry."

"Guess you'll have to learn."

"I don't want to learn," he protested. "I'm a rancher, not a cook." He gave her a wry smile. "I'm liable to poison the customers."

"Then I suggest you either close the diner down or hire someone to run it for you. Good luck, Austin."

Again she turned away from him and walked out of the barn, her head high as she crossed the yard toward the buckboard.

Austin hurried after her. He couldn't let her leave without hearing his plan. She might still leave and never speak to him again, but he had to at least try.

He caught up to her and grabbed the horse's bridle. "Will you just hold up a minute?"

"What do you want now? Haven't you taken enough from us?"

"You don't have to leave town. Your father can have the diner back."

A crease formed between her finely arched brows. "What? How?"

"Come and sit down on the porch and talk to me and I'll explain everything."

He released the bridle and moved to the side of the buckboard, holding his hand out to help her down. For a time, she looked as if she might refuse. Then finally, she rested her hand in his and climbed out.

Keeping her gloved hand in his, he led her across the yard and up the steps to the porch. He gestured to one of the rocking chairs. "Sit down for a minute."

She perched on the edge of the chair, while Austin leaned his hips on the railing in front of her.

"Austin," she said, "if this is one of your crazy schemes …"

It was. In fact, it was probably the craziest scheme he'd ever thought up. "No, it isn't. It's perfectly logical and rational."

"And this plan of yours means Papa can have the diner back?"

Austin nodded. She was coming around. He could hear the hope in her voice. And knowing how much she loved her father, he knew she'd do anything she could to help him out of the situation he'd gotten into. He was counting on that.

"That's right."

"How? He refused to take it back last night."

Austin shook his head. "I know. He said it would look like he'd welched on the bet. I tried to tell him that I'd make sure people knew the truth, but he wouldn't budge."

"Then how will you persuade him to take it back?"

"I won't," he replied. "You will."

"He won't listen to me."

"He will if you own the diner," he went on.

"Well, of course, but I don't own it. You do."

"You can own it."

"Now I know you've lost your mind. In the first place, I can't afford to buy it from you." She rose to her feet and made to move past him. "In the second place—"

"You don't need money to own it," he said. His heartbeat thundered in his chest. This was it. Everything he'd ever wanted was within his reach—or his relationship with Chloe would be destroyed for good. "All you have to do is marry me."

CHAPTER 3

*C*hloe couldn't have heard him right. She thought she'd heard him ask her to marry him, but that was impossible. They weren't courting. They weren't even real friends now. "What did you say?"

He reached out and took her hands in his. Through her lace gloves, his warmth snaked up her arms, making her entire body heat. Mercy me, she thought, gazing into his eyes, wondering if he'd felt the same unusual feeling.

"I … I want you to marry me," Austin repeated.

She was stunned. Speechless. While birds soared overhead in the cloudless sky and in the distance a horse neighed, all she could do was stare at Austin, trying to make sense of what he'd said. Finally, the only thing she could think of to say was, "Why would I want to do that?"

He chuckled then, trying to make the moment light. "Because you can't resist me?"

She sent him a disparaging glance.

"Because I want to help you."

"How is marrying me going to help?"

"If we're married, I can give you the diner as a wedding gift. You can then do what you want with it. You can either give it back to your father, if he'll take it, or you can ask him to just run it for you."

"That's the most ridiculous idea I've ever heard," she sputtered.

He shrugged. "Ridiculous ideas sometimes change the world," he countered. "I'm sure steam engines and the telegraph were ridiculous ideas at one time, too."

"Marriage is not an invention," she pointed out. "It's a lifetime commitment, and one I'm not willing to make."

"You don't ever want to marry and have a family?"

She shook her head. "You know I've always dreamed of leaving Rocky Ridge, of seeing the world."

"I remember you used to talk about that all the time. You still feel the same way?"

She nodded. "And I refuse to let a man control me. It seems that's a woman's lot as soon as she becomes a wife."

"It doesn't have to be that way."

"Maybe not, but I'm not willing to risk it." Her

brow furrowed. "Why would you even suggest such a thing as marriage? What do you get out of it?"

"Nothing," he lied.

"Nobody does anything for nothing."

"We're friends, right?"

They hadn't been close for years, but obviously he either didn't realize that or was ignoring it. "Yes," she conceded. "We're friends."

"You need help."

"Marrying someone is more than 'helping'. It's forever. I'm sure there are dozens of unmarried women in town who'd be happy to marry you."

"That's the problem, and that's why this is the perfect solution," he said. He was perfectly capable of avoiding marriage to any of the single ladies in town by himself, but if he could use that as a way to convince Chloe to marry him, he would.

"What do you mean?"

"It's getting I'm afraid to go into town because I'll be accosted by mamas trying to foist their daughters off on me just because I'm single."

"I'm sure it's not as bad as you think."

His brows lifted. "It's worse," he protested. "Why, just last week I was in the barber's shop getting a haircut and a shave when Rosemary Masters and her daughter came in to invite me to supper."

Chloe couldn't prevent a chuckle from escaping. "What did you say?"

"I said no, of course. Can you imagine being married to a woman who'd track me down no matter where I was? She'd be like a hound dog, likely even follow me to the outhouse if she'd a mind to."

"Knowing Daisy Masters, I have no doubt you're right."

"I'm tired of it, Chloe. Tired of mamas trying to marry me off to their daughters. It's not as if they care about me at all. They're only interested in the ranch and my name."

"I suppose that could be true."

"It is. You and I have known each other since we were kids. I know I can trust you, and I know you're not interested in my family's money or standing in the community. I want to marry somebody I already know I like and get along with. Like you said, nobody does anything for nothing. So yes, I am getting something. What I get out of it is peace. So just think about it. There's no rush for you to leave."

"I ..." She couldn't possibly even consider doing something so ... permanent. "Supposing I agree to this lunacy and it doesn't work out. Then what? Do you take the diner back?"

He shook his head. "The diner will always be yours from the day we get married, but on one condition."

"Which is?"

"If I ever hear of your father gambling again, I'll take it back. You'd have to make sure he understands that."

"That seems fair."

"Besides," he went on. "It won't be an issue. I'll make you happy enough that it'll work. I promise."

"It's a crazy idea …"

"I'm pretty easy to get along with," he said with a grin. "I bathe regularly, I don't snore, and I'll eat just about anything that's put in front of me."

Chloe couldn't help but laugh. If those were the only requirements she had for a husband, she was sure there were several men in town who would fit the bill. She and Austin did get along well, she mused. They used to have fun together. And he was handsome, she'd give him that. She'd have financial security for the rest of her life, as well.

"It would solve your father's problems," he persisted.

No, she couldn't marry him. The idea was ludicrous. Marriage to any man would destroy all her carefully laid-out plans for her future.

Marriage to Austin would mean living on the Bar-W. Not that it would be a hardship, she mused. The ranch house was spacious and elegant, and reminded her of the photos she'd seen of the mansions in cities like New York and Philadelphia.

But no, she couldn't do it. If she ever married—which she had no plans to—she'd marry for love. Nothing less.

She liked Austin. Always had, at least until she was about fourteen and suddenly, whenever she was around him, she became shy and tongue-tied, and her insides did a strange little dance that made her feel both feverish and chilled at the same time.

She'd stopped spending time with him and had started making excuses to avoid him whenever possible.

Even today, when she'd thought she was mature enough to deal with him, those same sensations filled her.

Mercy, being married to him would mean a lifetime of being on edge every second, of her nerve endings tingling uncontrollably.

"No," she said. "It's a crazy idea, and I just ... can't."

She couldn't meet his gaze, couldn't stand to see the disappointment in his dark eyes. Without another word, she hurried down the porch steps and raced across the yard to the buckboard. She climbed up, and as she picked up the reins, she shifted to face him one last time. "I do appreciate the offer, and if I was in the market for a husband, you'd be my first choice. But—"

"Think about it, Chloe. Promise me you'll think about it."

She looked up at him, seeing—what was that expression on his face? Why was this so important to him? She'd seen how women swarmed around him no matter where they were, but surely that couldn't be the only reason he was being so persistent. Yet she couldn't think of any other possible motive for what he was suggesting.

She shook her head. "There's really nothing to think about."

"Please …"

Her throat tightened. She hadn't realized until right this second just how much she'd miss him once she left town. "Fine. I'll think about it, but I won't change my mind."

"Stand still or you're going to fall off the chair." Hattie McGuigan, Chloe's best friend, folded the hem of the lilac skirt and slid another pin into place.

Chloe should be at the diner, packing, but when Hattie had begged her to come and visit for a while, she hadn't been able to resist. Besides, who would help her hem her dresses once she was living … she didn't know where?

"Sorry," Chloe muttered. "Will you be much longer?"

"Just about done," Hattie told her, "but if you don't stop fidgeting, the hem will have more curves than Alice Duguid."

Giggles erupted. It was a well-known fact that Alice was overly … endowed … but had the tiniest waist of any woman in town.

Hattie plucked another pin from the heart-shaped pin cushion attached to her wrist, "but maybe I should take my time. I don't want you to move away."

Chloe didn't want to move either. She'd grown up

in Rocky Ridge and even though she couldn't wait to leave and see the rest of the world, she'd always thought she'd one day come back home and settle down. She couldn't imagine growing old anywhere else.

Still, now she had no choice. There was no work here for her father, and she doubted Austin would keep the diner open. Even if he did, her father would have far too much pride to work for him.

Chloe had spent the past half hour talking to Hattie, trying to curb her tears as she went over every detail of the night that had changed everything as well as Austin's proposition the next day.

The poker game had been the biggest news to hit Rocky Ridge in months. Hattie had heard about it, but hadn't heard Chloe's account of the events after Elvin and Austin left the saloon.

Chloe always counted on Hattie to be the voice of reason, while at the same time, she always managed to brighten Chloe's day and stop her from taking life so seriously. What would she ever do without her to talk to, without her shoulder to cry on when she needed it, without her sense of adventure and fun?

"I don't want to leave either, but we have no choice," she said. "My only other option is to marry Austin and then somehow convince my father to take the diner back."

"So marry him," Hattie begged.

"I told you, I can't do that," Chloe protested.

Hattie threaded the last pin through the fabric.

"Sure you can," she contradicted. "You like him, don't you?"

"Of course I like him." Chloe carefully climbed down off the chair. "I always have, but he makes me … uncomfortable now."

Hattie grinned. "Maybe you like him a bit more than you want to admit."

"I do not!"

Hattie waved her objection away. "Doesn't matter. You could still marry him and get everything you want."

Chloe recognized the glint in Hattie's eyes. "What is going through that mind of yours?"

Hattie grinned. "A plan."

Chloe wasn't sure she wanted to hear what Hattie had in mind. Hattie's "plans" had gotten her into trouble so many times while they were growing up. The worst was when Hattie had assured her that smoking one of her father's cigars was a good idea.

It wasn't. She still felt queasy whenever she thought about it.

Now, though, Chloe was desperate for a solution. "What's your plan?" she asked, letting the skirt drop to the floor and stepping out of it. Hattie picked it up and draped it over the back of the chair.

"Well," Hattie began, "the diner is yours as soon as you marry him, right?"

Chloe nodded.

"No matter what happens after that?"

"Y-e—s." Chloe could almost see the wheels turning in Hattie's brain. "So?"

"So, even if you end up hating each other, you'd still have the diner."

"That's what he said," Chloe reminded her.

Hattie grinned. "Then it's very simple. You marry him, get the diner and then leave him."

"What?" Chloe couldn't believe her best friend would even suggest something so horrible. Hattie was the kindest, most compassionate person she'd ever known. "You can't be serious."

Hattie shrugged. "I admit it's not very nice—"

"Not very nice?" Chloe repeated. "That's the most underhanded thing I've ever heard. I'm shocked you could even think of something like that."

Hattie gave Chloe a wry smile. "I didn't," she told her. "I read about a woman in Ohio who did something similar to her husband to get access to an inheritance he'd received. She gradually stole the money and hid it, then when she had it all, she left him. It wasn't until she died a few months later that they found the money hidden in the small house she'd bought in Tennessee."

"How cruel," Chloe breathed.

Hattie nodded in agreement. "If she hadn't died, she would have lived comfortably for the rest of her life."

"And you think I should do something like that to Austin?"

Hattie sighed. "No, Austin is too nice." She slid

the pin cushion off her wrist and put it back in the sewing basket.

"I couldn't hurt him like that," Chloe said.

"Well, there is one other way … You could make his life miserable until he can't wait to get rid of you. Then you'd still have the diner, and you'd be free to continue with your own plans. He wouldn't be hurt because he would hate you." Hattie grinned. "You're welcome."

"What?" This idea was even worse than her original plan. "I couldn't possibly—"

"I'd never suggest doing something so cruel if there was any other solution, but I can't think of one."

"I can't either."

"You know, being married to Austin might not be as bad as you think. You might actually get to like it."

Chloe chuckled then. "That would never happen in a million years."

"Never say never. He's quite a catch."

"I'm not fishing," Chloe reminded her.

"Nevertheless, if a fish jumped in your boat, would you really throw it back when you need food?"

All the way home that afternoon, Chloe replayed her conversation with Hattie. Could she really marry Austin and treat him so badly that he'd ask her to leave?

No, she decided, she most definitely couldn't. She just had to come up with another way to get the diner back without marrying him.

CHAPTER 4

Chloe's father was sitting at one of the tables in the diner when she got back from the Hattie's later that afternoon. His shoulders were hunched, his head drooping, and his hands wrapped around a mug of coffee.

He looked up at her through bloodshot eyes when the bell above the door jangled and she walked in.

Never had she seen such misery in a person's eyes.

"Where've you been?" he asked.

"Hattie's," she replied.

He nodded and lowered his head to study the coffee in his mug. "I'm sorry, poppet," he muttered. "So sorry."

She wanted to be angry, to rail at him for gambling again, for destroying their future. But what would be the point? It was done. He'd gambled away their livelihood, and now they had to figure out how to survive.

She crossed the dining room and slid into the chair beside him, then reached out and covered his hand with hers. "I know, Papa."

"I've ruined everything. I don't know what we're going to do now. We have nothing left because of me."

"We'll be all right," Chloe said, doing her best to sound as cheerful and positive as she could.

"Not this time." He got to his feet. "No, not this time."

Chloe watched him trudge across the room and disappear into the kitchen. Moments later, she heard his footsteps on the stairs.

She'd never seen him so … defeated. Lost.

What could she do? What would they do? She'd told Austin they'd be out of the diner in a few days, but they had nowhere to go. She had her savings, so they could survive for a little while, but then what? They had no future.

Unless … unless she married Austin.

He'd promised to give her the diner if she married him, and she didn't doubt his word. Her father would refuse to let her give it to him, but once she pointed out it was *her* diner and she needed him to keep it open for her, he'd accept it. His life would go back to normal. He'd have to hire someone to help him since she'd be living at the Bar-W, but that was a minor inconvenience.

As she carried his coffee mug back to the kitchen and tidied the mess he'd made, the notion rolled around in her mind.

Austin was a good man. She knew that. She could do worse. She just hadn't intended to marry, at least not in the near future.

She went upstairs to her bedroom and closed the door behind her. She slumped onto the side of the bed and stared at the bookshelf. California, New York City, England, France ... The books taunted her.

If she married Austin, she'd have to give up all her dreams of traveling around the world.

A sound carried through the wall from her father's bedroom. A sob? It couldn't be, could it? Men didn't cry. Yet that's what it sounded like. Was it possible this man who'd always been a source of strength to her was crying?

Could she really be so selfish as to think of herself when the most important person in her life was suffering so badly?

Austin exited the mercantile, pausing on the boardwalk as two elderly ladies crossed his path. He tipped his hat and bid them good morning before continuing toward the wagon sitting in front of the store.

Automatically, the same way he found himself doing every time he came to town, he looked down the street in the direction of Millie's Diner, hoping to catch sight of Chloe coming or going.

It had been four days since Chloe had turned

down his proposal, and he couldn't help wondering if she and Elvin had already left town. There would be no reason for them to tell him when they were leaving.

He owned Millie's Diner now, and if Chloe and Elvin were already gone, it only made sense that he take a ride down there to check that the building was locked up.

His gut twisted painfully at the thought that Chloe might have already left and he'd never see her again.

He climbed into the wagon and picked up the reins. Then, as if he'd conjured her up through some sort of magic, Chloe appeared in the diner's doorway. She stood in the entrance for a few moments and scanned the street.

She was too far away for him to see the details of her face, but he didn't need to. He'd memorized every detail, from the long dark lashes that fanned her cheeks when she closed her eyes to the tiny mole beside her left eye to the rosy lips she nibbled on when she was thinking. He could see the light blue dress she was wearing, how it showed off her small but perfect curves, and how the reddish tones in her dark brown hair glistened in the sunshine.

She looked in his direction, and he sensed when her gaze landed on him. Heat rushed through him. Then she moved, and he watched as she strode purposefully across the street and down the boardwalk toward him.

He was mesmerized by the movement of her hips, the way her dainty hand clasped the handle of the basket she was carrying. He couldn't help noticing how she paused and greeted everyone she passed with a smile. She was a beautiful woman, inside and out.

"Good morning, Austin," she said when she finally reached him and stopped to look up at him sitting on the seat in the wagon.

He met her gaze. "Morning, Chloe," he replied. "How are you and your father doing?"

She ignored his question. "I'm glad you happened to be in town today," she said. "Can we talk?"

What could she possibly want to talk to him about? She'd made it clear she wasn't interested in his proposition. He couldn't think of any other business she might have with him, though. "Of course."

He climbed down out of the wagon and cupped her elbow, leading her away from the wagon and the people in front of the general store. "Are you in a hurry? I was just about to have some lunch at the hotel. We can talk there if you'd care to join me."

She smiled. "I'd like that."

They didn't speak while they made their way down the street to the Grand Hotel and stepped inside. Howard Marsh, the hotel's owner, greeted them. "Is your dining room open for lunch?" Austin asked.

"It is," Mr. Marsh replied, gesturing for them to follow him. He led them into a large airy room with windows looking out onto the street. Several tables with snowy white tablecloths and vases of fresh flowers dotted the space. "Will this table be satisfactory?" he asked, stopping in front of a table by the window. "It's fine, thanks," Austin replied, then held a chair for Chloe to sit down.

Austin took the chair directly opposite her.

As soon as Mr. Marsh left, a waiter approached and offered them menus. "May I get you something to drink while you decide?" he asked.

Austin raised his brows in Chloe's direction. "Just water, please," she said quietly.

"Water for both of us, thanks."

With a barely noticeable bow, the waiter retreated, returning shortly with two glasses of water.

"The roast beef here is good," Austin commented after the waiter left again, sneaking a glance at Chloe as she studied the menu, a few tiny frown lines on her forehead.

"I haven't eaten here before," she said. "Naturally, I always ate at the diner."

Austin leaned closer to whisper. "Don't tell Mr. Marsh, but while the food here is good, I always preferred the diner's."

Her lips quirked in a half-smile. "You were always one of our best customers."

Did she have any idea why he was such a good customer? Yes, the food there was excellent, but even if it had tasted like sawdust, he would still have gone there just to see Chloe.

Austin closed his menu and put it on the table beside him. "Have you decided what you'd like?"

Chloe nodded, closing her menu and setting it on top of Austin's.

Seconds later, the waiter approached their table and Austin placed their order.

The only other customers in the dining room rose and walked out, leaving Austin and Chloe alone.

She avoided his gaze, her eyes focusing on the goings-on outside. Two children were playing nearby, their laughter seeping into the silence between them.

Austin didn't want to ask why she wanted to speak to him, but he couldn't help wondering. "Chloe?"

She turned to face him, her expression serious. She rested her hands on the table.

Austin noticed she seemed nervous. Why? They'd always been able to talk about anything without reservation.

"I suppose you're wondering what I wanted to talk to you about," she said finally.

Austin nodded. "Take your time. I can wait until you're ready."

"It's about … I mean, you … you mentioned getting married …"

Austin's heartbeat fluttered and he held his breath. Was it possible …? "As you know, it did cross my mind."

"I've been thinking about it as you asked me to," she went on.

"And?"

She looked down at her hands for a moment, and Austin waited, his nerves on edge. When she raised her head and met his gaze, it was obvious she was struggling to find the right words. "If you're still willing ... I'll marry you."

CHAPTER 5

*C*hloe's stomach tightened into a knot as the words left her lips.

They were out in the open now. She'd agreed to marry Austin, and the life she'd planned for herself was gone.

She watched his expression. His lips curved in a huge smile and his eyes filled with happiness. For a moment or two, she was afraid he was actually going to let out a whoop of joy the way he used to when he was a boy.

Luckily, he controlled himself. Instead, he took her hands in his. "That's good to hear," he said. "You won't be sorry. I promise you that."

She was already sorry, but she bit her tongue before the words spilled out. "I do have one condition," she said after a few seconds.

The happiness faded from his eyes, and frown lines appeared. "What's that?"

"I don't want my father—and everyone else in town—to know the circumstances of our marriage. I'd like them all to think we're in love."

"You don't think they're going to catch on, since we haven't been courting?"

She shook her head. "I think my father will want to believe that because we've been friends for so long that it's a natural progression. As for everyone else, I'm sure they'll think we've been keeping company quietly."

"Considering the circumstances, do you think your father will approve?"

She nodded. "He always liked you and respected you, and even now, I don't think that's changed. He'll be happy to see me married off, especially to the most eligible bachelor in town."

"You do realize that in order to appear like a couple in love, we'll have to spend time together and show affection like every other engaged and newly married couple."

Mercy, she hadn't even stopped to consider that. Although times were changing, she still believed it wasn't proper to touch each other in public, but she wondered if she'd be able to convincingly pretend she was in love.

She nodded shyly as she picked up the linen napkin on the table and began to twist the corner between her fingers.

"I promise I won't ravish you in public," he teased.

Her head lifted, her eyes wide. "Austin!"

He laughed. "I'm happy to accept your terms, but there is one other thing we need to talk about …"

"Oh?" Her brows lifted. She'd agreed to marry him. What more could he possibly want from her?

He leaned closer and reached out, resting his hand on hers. "This is forever for me," he said.

Forever! He expected forever. Guilt washed over her. If she followed through with Hattie's plan, his forever wouldn't last more than a few months.

"I want a real marriage," he went on, "if you know what I mean."

Heat rose in her cheeks. "Oh …"

Heavens! He wanted to … She'd heard bits of pieces of what happened between husbands and wives in the marriage bed, but it had all sounded very confusing and unpleasant. It hadn't even occurred to her that Austin would expect to claim his marital rights.

"Apparently you do know," he added.

He'd obviously noticed the flush she felt rising in her cheeks.

"I want children," he went on, "and as far as I know, there's only one way to get them. You do understand that, don't you?"

"This isn't a proper discussion—" What if someone overheard them?

"If we're going to be married, it's something we have to discuss. It's important to me."

"I see."

At that moment, the waiter returned carrying a tray. He set the plate of roast beef in front of Austin, and a chicken pot pie in front of Chloe.

"Enjoy your meal, folks," he said, then turned and left them alone.

"Well?" Austin asked once he was out of earshot. "What do you think?"

She took a small bite of the pot pie. "I think the chicken in this pie is a bit overcooked. It's a little dry."

"I mean about what I asked."

"I know what you meant," she said, keeping her gaze leveled on her food. "I don't quite know how to answer. I don't have any experience with … that kind of …"

"I understand that, and to be honest, that pleases me."

"I'm sure my mother planned to explain about … that … when I got married, but she didn't get the chance to." She paused, taking in a calming breath. and releasing it slowly. "If that's what you expect, and if you have patience with me, I'll do my best to please you."

If she only knew, Austin thought. Just being able to wake up beside her every morning would please him. Knowing she was waiting for him every evening would please him. Hell, everything she did pleased him. Having her in his bed, and making love with her would do more than please him. "You don't have to do anything to please me, Chloe. And I hope I can please you, too."

Her eyes widened. "Austin! That's …" She looked around guiltily, hoping no one could hear their conversation. "Please!"

Austin chuckled. "I'm sorry, Chloe. I don't mean to embarrass you."

"Then stop talking and eat your food."

He held up his hands in mock surrender. "We'll talk about it another time. Now, what about our wedding? I think it's best that we get married as soon as possible. I heard your father closed the diner that night and hasn't opened it since."

"That's right," she replied. "He hasn't. He's barely been out of bed, and even though I've tried to tempt him with his favorite meals, he's hardly eaten anything."

"Then we need to hurry so he can get the diner back up and running. If it's all right with you, I'll go and see the pastor this afternoon. We could get married at his house, but I assume you'd like to be married in church. After all, it is the only wedding we'll ever have."

Chloe nodded. It would be the only wedding she'd ever have. She had no intentions of ever marrying again once he divorced her. "Yes, I'd like it to be in church."

Edith Worsley, a woman Austin recognized from the ladies' society his mother had belonged to before she passed, appeared in the entrance to the dining room. Her daughter, Ann, stood behind her, as if she were trying to be invisible. Mr. Marsh stood off to the side, menus in hand.

Austin watched as Mrs. Worsley turned her head and whispered something to Ann. She patted Ann's arm and left her standing alone while she marched across the room to his table. Mr. Marsh escorted Ann to a table at the opposite end of the room.

Austin stood up as she approached. "Hello, Mrs. Worsley."

"Good morning, Austin," she said. "It's nice to see you again. You haven't been in town much lately."

"I've been pretty busy," he commented.

"And how is your brother?"

"He's just fine, thanks for asking."

"I'm so glad to run into you today. It saves me having to send a message out to the ranch. I'm having a small dinner party on Saturday evening. I'd be honored if you and your brother would attend."

Out of the corner of his eye, he saw Ann Worsley subtly watching them.

"I can't speak for Jamie but I'm sure if he doesn't have any prior engagements, he'd love to."

"That's wonderful," she gushed. "And you?"

He reached over and took Chloe's hand in his. "I'm sorry, Chloe and I have other plans." He grinned at Chloe, then turned back to Mrs. Worsley. "Oh, of course you know my fiancé, Chloe, don't you?"

Mrs. Worsley's eyes widened. "Fiancé?" she sputtered.

Austin nodded, grinning. "That's right. Chloe has

just consented to become my wife, so we're having a celebratory lunch before we go and make arrangements with the pastor."

"Oh … well … I …" Mrs. Worsley blustered. "I mean, congratulations …"

Chloe gave Mrs. Worsley a sweet smile. "Thank you. I hope you and Ann can come to the ceremony."

"Of course … well, if you'll excuse me, I must go …"

"So nice to see you again," Austin called out to the woman's retreating back.

Once Mrs. Worsley was back at her own table, Chloe leaned forward, resting her elbows on the table. "How rude! To interrupt and invite you to supper when it's obvious what she's trying to do—"

"See what I mean?" he commented. "I can't even have lunch—"

Chloe giggled. "It is a curse, I imagine."

"It is," Austin said. Mrs. Worsley's interruption couldn't have come at a better time. He'd wondered if Chloe really believed his motives for asking her to marry him, and Mrs. Worsley had managed to help him without even realizing it. "You're saving me from the clutches of every spinster in town. Now, finish your meal and we'll go and tell your father the news before Mrs. Worsley has a chance to set tongues wagging. I'm sure everyone in town will know about our upcoming nuptials before we even finish dessert."

～

Chloe slipped her arms into the cream silk gown trimmed with silk bows and ribbon.

It was her wedding day. In a few hours, she would be Mrs. Austin Hayward and the life she'd planned for herself would be gone—at least temporarily. If she could force herself to follow Hattie's plan … She wouldn't think about that now.

"It's such a beautiful dress," Hattie commented. "I'm glad you decided to wear it. Your mama would be so pleased."

Chloe nodded. "As soon as I tried it on, I felt her presence with me."

While Chloe tried to calm the thousands of butterflies flitting around in her stomach, Hattie fastened the row of pearl buttons down the back of the dress.

"Now for the veil." Hattie picked up the lace veil and arranged it on Chloe's curls. Then she stood back and clasped her hands together. "Stunning," she breathed. "Absolutely stunning."

Chloe carefully crossed the room to the mirror standing in the corner. She gazed at her reflection, her throat tightening. A tear escaped and trickled down her cheek. Yes, she thought, her mother would be pleased.

A sudden knock at the door startled her. "Are you ready, poppet? It's time."

"Yes, Papa."

Chloe turned to Hattie, who grabbed her and

hugged her tightly. "No matter how this ends up, you know you can count on me."

"I know," Chloe replied through the thickness in her throat.

Hattie opened the door and stepped aside. "Then let's go get you married."

CHAPTER 6

*A*ustin paced the pastor's office in the small church, taking out the pocket watch that had once belonged to his grandfather.

"You just checked the time," Jamie pointed out.

Austin clasped the watch for the fourth time in as many minutes. "I'm checking it again."

What if Chloe changed her mind? What if she was leaving town right this minute? What if—?

The rattle of wagon wheels and the jingle of harness floated through the open window. Austin was about to look out to see if it was Chloe when Jamie grabbed his arm and pulled him back inside.

"It's unlucky to see the bride before the wedding," Jamie reminded him. "Let me look."

Austin nodded. He wasn't about to let anything, even superstition, prevent him from marrying Chloe if he could help it.

"It's her," Jamie said, grinning as he looked out the window. "So we'd best get out there."

As he spoke, a knock came to the door and the pastor walked in. "Ready, son?" he asked.

A few minutes later, Austin waited at the front of the church for Chloe and her father to come down the aisle and meet him at the altar. He'd fantasized about this day for so long that he couldn't believe it was really going to happen.

The door to the church opened and Chloe and her father walked in.

Austin couldn't contain the gasp that escaped his lips. An angel—his angel—stood in the doorway, framed by the sunshine streaming in around her.

He forgot to breathe. His heartbeat raced and his throat thickened with emotion as he watched her walk toward him.

Her fingers trembled when they joined hands and the pastor began the ceremony, so he gave her hand a gentle squeeze of reassurance.

A few minutes later, the vows were said, and they were man and wife.

Austin's heart felt as if it might explode with happiness.

"You can kiss your bride now, Austin," the pastor said, grinning.

He gazed at Chloe, his heart bursting with love for this woman who was now legally his wife. He'd give anything to wrap his arms around her and kiss her senseless, but he managed to control himself. Hopefully, one day he'd be able to kiss her the way he dreamed of and she'd respond the same way. For now, he'd have to be gentle and patient.

He spoke quietly, hoping his voice was soft enough that the pastor wouldn't be able to hear him. "It's not fatal, or if it is, I'm doing it wrong."

He smiled at her. She nodded a moment before he lowered his head to hers. He grazed her lips softly, barely touching them, but it was enough to make him almost groan with the intensity of his desire for her.

He forced himself to pull away before he scared her. As it was, when he met her gaze, she was looking at him with a dazed expression on her face, as if she'd never seen him before. It was disconcerting, to say the least.

"Congratulations!" The pastor's voice broke into the moment, and within seconds, he and Chloe were surrounded by friends and family wishing them well.

Austin was well aware this wedding was not what Chloe wanted, but he hoped that in time, she'd come to love him even half as much as he loved her.

Chloe's heartbeat tripped as Austin closed the door, shutting them off from the rest of the world.

They were alone. Completely alone in the largest and most elegant room in the Grand Hotel.

"You don't mind spending the night here, do you?" he asked, crossing to a table near the window where Mr. Marsh had set up a chilled bottle of champagne and two glasses. "I should have asked you first, I guess."

"It's fine."

"I thought you might be too tired to ride out to the ranch tonight. You've had a long day."

It had been a very long and tiring day. After the ceremony, the ladies in town had provided a wedding feast for them, with toasts to their happiness, dancing and laughter.

Normally, she would have thoroughly enjoyed herself, but all afternoon, the only thing she could think about was her reaction to Austin's kiss.

Many times during the wedding feast, she'd caught herself staring at Austin's lips, wondering what it was about his kiss that had affected her so much. It was a mere brush of his lips against hers, but it had caused her to feel light-headed for a few seconds, as if she might swoon. The most unusual sensations had swept through her body and her heart had fluttered inside her chest.

Austin's voice dragged her thoughts away from the kiss and back to the present. "I thought it would be nice to have some time by ourselves."

"Why?" she asked. "We've been by ourselves lots of times."

He chuckled. "Not as married folks."

Then she remembered, and her cheeks flamed. This was where she and Hattie had decided she should put her plan to make him regret marrying her into action.

She'd agreed to a true marriage in all ways, and he would be angry at her sudden reversal. That was the plan.

Yet all afternoon and evening, she couldn't help thinking about the way his kiss after the wedding had ignited something inside her, something foreign, but so exciting.

If a chaste kiss could be so thrilling, what would a real kiss—and more—do? Heaven help her, she wanted to find out.

Surely it couldn't hurt to wait until tomorrow to start making him miserable, she thought.

Austin closed the gap between them. Tenderly, he clasped her shoulders and drew her into his arms, wrapping them around her and holding her against his chest. A woodsy scent she'd always associated with him wafted around her. She could hear his heartbeat, strong and steady. "I promise you I'll do everything I can to make you happy."

If he only knew that it didn't matter what he did, she wouldn't be happy. If he only knew that by the time their marriage ended, he'd be the one who'd be happy—happy to be rid of her.

He released her and held her at arms' length. "I know this seems a bit awkward," he said. "We've been friends for so long, but I've never kissed you before."

"At the wedding—"

"I mean a real kiss, the kind of kiss a husband gives his wife. I really want to do that right now."

"Oh …" Chloe felt her face flame, and she couldn't meet his gaze.

"I'll wait, though, because if I start kissing you now, I won't be able to stop. So I'm going downstairs for a little while to give you some privacy while you get ready for bed. How long do you think you'll need?"

Forever, she was tempted to say. "A half hour?"

"You're sure?"

She nodded. "Why?"

"Looks like it might take that long just to get yourself out of that dress."

She hadn't thought of that. The row of buttons running down the back of her gown would be a problem. "You're right," she said. She had no choice but to ask him to help.

Turning her back on him, she murmured, "Do you mind?"

"Not at all."

Chloe heard the amusement in his voice, and moments later, his fingers grazed her skin. Her breath was trapped in her throat, and every nerve ending tingled under his touch.

Suddenly, his touch was gone, and a chill settled on her bare back.

"All done," he said.

Was it her imagination that his voice had deepened when he spoke?

The door opened and before she could turn around, it closed behind him.

Austin sat on one of the stuffed armchairs in the hotel lobby, his thoughts drifting to the woman waiting for him upstairs.

His wife.

The woman he'd wanted for all of his adult life was now his.

Guilt jabbed at him at the way he'd practically forced her to marry him, though. He'd been greedy, thinking only of himself. He hadn't stopped to consider what she'd had to sacrifice.

He'd taken away her dream of seeing the world, and that weighed heavily on him.

Since she was a girl, she'd regaled him with stories of Europe and Asia, of the places she wanted to see, the things she wanted to do. She'd shown him the books she'd bought and the photographs she'd pored over for hours at a time.

He liked her as a person, and loved her as a woman. He could think of nothing that would make him happier than to take care of her, to raise a family with her, to grow old with her by his side. And to have her in his bed.

His body ached with need to be with her in every sense. She'd agreed to a real marriage, but it had been plain to see she'd rather lie naked in a bed of thorns.

He had rights. Legal rights. But rights or not, he couldn't bring himself to take advantage of the woman he loved.

He took his pocket watch out and glanced at the time. He got up and crossed the lobby to the stairs. The sooner he told her his decision, the better.

Chloe stood in front of the dresser and looked at her reflection in the mirror as she finished braiding her hair. Holding the braid in one hand, she picked up the pale yellow ribbon from the dresser, then wound it around the braid and tied it.

She was ready. She'd changed into the white cotton nightgown Hattie had made her and now there was nothing else for her to do but wait for Austin to come back.

She swallowed thickly and took in several deep breaths to calm the fluttering in her stomach. Her heart skittered in her ribs, and her whole body trembled in fear.

She wasn't afraid, she repeated for the umpteenth time. There was no reason to be afraid. Women submitted to their husbands every day.

But this was Austin! Austin, the boy she'd played games with, the boy she'd fished with, the boy who had been her partner in the three-legged race at the Fourth of July celebration the year she turned fifteen.

He would never hurt her, though. She knew that. She trusted him completely.

They'd shared one brief kiss that had created such sensations in her that she couldn't imagine what anything more might do. Yet she found herself curious, and even a little eager to find out what went on between a man and a woman in the marriage bed.

She was nervous. She was inexperienced. She was hesitant.

But she was not afraid. And if she kept telling herself that, maybe by the time Austin returned, she'd believe it.

She was about to climb into bed and try to sleep when the door opened.

She spun around. Austin came into the room and paused, closing the door quietly behind him.

Heat rose in her cheeks. "You were gone a long time," she commented.

"I know." He took off his jacket and hung it on the back of a chair.

Awkward silence filled the room.

Finally, he crossed to where she was standing and took one of her hands in his.

The pleasant sensation of his work-roughened hands against her smooth skin surprised her.

"I've made a decision," he said quietly.

The seriousness in his dark eyes worried her. Did he regret marrying her already? "What is it?"

"I told you I want a real marriage and you agreed …"

Her heart thumped in her chest. Her breath stalled in her throat. "I did."

"But I've decided that I'm going to wait until you want a real marriage as much as I do."

She should be relieved, so why did she feel a little … disappointed? What was wrong with her? "You have the right—"

"I know that, and believe me, it's tempting, but I want our marriage to start off right. What kind of husband would I be if I forced you to do something you're not ready for? I've never forced a woman yet, and I don't intend to start now, especially with the woman I vowed to love, honor and cherish for the rest of my life."

Chloe's admiration for Austin grew even higher than it already was. He really was the kindest man she'd ever known. If she wanted a husband, she'd consider herself very lucky to be married to him.

She should be thankful he didn't expect to exercise his marital rights. Instead, she couldn't help wondering what had changed his mind.

Before she had time to think about it further, he reached out and untied the ribbon holding her braid in place.

"What are you doing?"

"Now that we're married, I'd really like to see your hair down." He slid his fingers into the braid and worked it loose until her hair hung in curls and waves around her shoulders.

"You've seen my hair down before," she pointed out.

"Not since you were a girl."

She realized that was true. When she was working in the diner, she kept it pulled back in a severe bun at the nape of her neck. When she went out socially, it was usually pinned away from her face.

"You have such beautiful hair," he said, wrapping its length around his hand.

She blushed. "Thank you."

"I want to kiss you right now." His voice was low and gruff. "A real kiss."

Chloe's heart raced in anticipation. "I think that would be all right."

"I'm glad to hear that."

With his hand still wrapped in her hair, he slid his other hand around her waist and urged her closer until their bodies were touching.

She held her breath as his lips lowered to hers and brushed against hers for a moment before he drew back.

Her eyes met his, and the desire in his dark depths stunned her. That he was denying himself something he so obviously wanted did something to her insides. Warmth seeped through her and her entire body tingled.

Then his mouth returned to meet hers, the pressure of his lips stronger, his arm tightening around her. His tongue traced the seam of her lips, and when she began to ask him why, it slipped inside.

An exquisite sensation burst inside her when his tongue stroked against hers. A boldness she'd never known overcame her and she met his movements, her tongue tangling with his, her arms snaking around his neck, her fingers combing through his hair.

A low moan sounded in the silence. His? Or hers? She didn't know.

Finally, he released her mouth, his breath coming in ragged gasps to match hers as he held her close to his chest. "I don't think we should do that too often," he croaked.

Chloe couldn't do anything but nod. Her knees were almost buckling, her heart racing and her throat too dry to speak.

She didn't know how long they stood clasped in each other's arms, but finally, he drew away. "We'd better get some sleep," he said, "although I'm pretty sure I should be taking a dip in the river first."

She wasn't sure why he'd want to go swimming so late at night, but she assumed he had his reasons and didn't think she should ask.

She climbed into bed and turned her back to him. She could hear him moving around and she knew he was removing his shirt and pants.

The room plunged into darkness when he turned off the lantern. Moments later, the bed squeaked and shifted when he crawled into the bed and she felt him settle beside her.

"Goodnight, Mrs. Hayward," he said.

"Goodnight, Austin." Chloe's brows furrowed. She was not pleased that she almost liked the sound of her new name.

CHAPTER 7

Sunlight was streaming through the window when Chloe woke the next morning. For a few seconds, she forgot where she was, until she heard the soft snore coming from beside her.

Then she remembered. She was a married woman now. She shifted to her side and looked over at Austin. In his sleep, his long lashes fanned his cheeks. His hair fell in soft curls over his forehead, and his jaw was shadowed with stubble.

Her body tingled with the memory of his kiss the night before. She hated to admit it, but she'd liked it, and she'd hoped he'd kiss her again.

As if he sensed her watching him, his eyes opened and he smiled at her. "Good morning."

"Good morning."

"How did you sleep?" he asked.

"Fine," she lied. She'd spent the better part of the night listening to Austin's soft, even breathing. "You?"

"Good." He hoisted himself up on one elbow and looked past her to the clock on the bureau. "We've slept late. We're going to have to hurry now."

He bounded out of bed, the sudden movement jostling her. "It's going to be close to noon by the time you visit with your father and convince him to take the diner back, and I do need to get back to the ranch," he said as he quickly put on his pants. "Jamie's had to handle all the morning chores, and it's not fair to leave him to take care of everything all day."

Chloe hadn't even thought about that. On special occasions, her father had put a sign in the window telling customers they were closed for the day. That wasn't an option on a ranch. Animals still had to be fed and watered, and there were likely other chores that needed to be done every day no matter what else was happening.

And naturally, Austin's sense of fair play wouldn't allow him to take advantage of someone else, even for a good reason—like his wedding. His fairness was one of the qualities she'd always admired about him, and she was pleased to see he hadn't lost that as he grew up.

This would a good time to put Hattie's plan into action, she thought. She should whine about being too tired to get up. That would likely annoy him, wouldn't it? She opened her mouth to tell him she wasn't getting out of bed just yet, but she couldn't do it. She couldn't bring herself to complain, especially since she was sure he was just as exhausted as she was.

He perched on the edge of her side of the bed and took her hand in his. "You're likely worn out after yesterday, so when we get home, you can have a nice long nap. I'll tell Dorcas to make sure no one bothers you."

"I … thank you." What else could she say? It was as if he'd anticipated her objection to getting up so early.

"I'll go downstairs and order us some breakfast while you get dressed. How does that sound?"

She nodded, and after he brushed a light kiss on her lips, he left.

Chloe threw back the sheet and sat up, dangling her feet over the side of the bed. If only he wasn't so considerate, she grumbled to herself. How was she supposed to make his life miserable when he was so easy to get along with and so concerned about her comfort?

She'd have to try harder to look for things to find fault with.

As quickly as she could, she put on a pink day dress and matching jacket. She twisted her hair into a knot and pinned it into place, then packed her nightgown in her bag and put it beside Austin's on the bureau.

A key sat beside his bag, so she took it and locked the door behind her before going down the stairs to the dining room.

Austin smiled and stood up as she entered. "You look lovely," he said, holding a chair out for her.

As she sat down, a middle-aged woman carrying a silver tray approached the table. She put it down on the table beside them and filled a china cup with tea from a matching teapot. "Milk and sugar or lemon, Mrs. Hayward?" she asked.

"Lemon, please," Chloe replied.

The woman added a slice of lemon to the cup and set it in front of Chloe, then turned to Austin. "Your meal will be ready shortly. If there's anything else you need, please let me know."

With a short half-curtsy, the woman hurried away.

"You ordered tea for me," Chloe commented. "I expected coffee."

Austin frowned. "You'd rather have coffee?" He motioned to raise his hand to summon the waitress, but Chloe reached over to stop him.

"No," she replied with a chuckle. "I prefer tea in the morning, but how did you know?"

"I came to the diner one morning for coffee. You weren't open yet, but you let me in and we talked while you brewed some. You were drinking tea, and you mentioned you always have tea first thing."

"That was …" Two or three years ago, she remembered. Yet he'd remembered a small detail like that. "A long time ago."

"I suppose it was," he agreed, looking over her shoulder toward the kitchen. "Here comes breakfast. I hope you're hungry."

She was, but when the meal arrived at the table, her eyes widened in surprise. "Mercy, Austin, I can't possibly eat all this food."

His brows arched. "No? I seem to recall you putting away more food than your father at the Founder's Day picnic a few years ago."

"I was a growing girl then," she pointed out. "I'd be the size of Mr. McNalty's barn if I ate like that now."

"You'd be perfect, no matter what size you were."

Chloe felt the heat rise in her cheeks. "Flattery will get you nowhere."

"Can't blame me for trying," he said with a grin. "If it's not working, though, let's finish breakfast. While you go and visit with your father, I'll pick up some supplies at the mercantile and then we can get back to the ranch."

Chloe sat quietly on the seat as Austin drove the wagon out of town two hours later. It had taken longer to explain that she was now the legal owner of the diner, and that she needed his help to keep it open. Eventually, though, he'd given in, promising her that his gambling days were over.

She hoped this time he meant it, because she knew Austin well enough to know he didn't make idle threats or promises. If he heard about her father gambling again, he would take the diner back, and her sacrifice would have been for nothing.

She'd expected Austin to be annoyed that she'd taken so long, and in a way, she hoped he would be. It was what she wanted, wasn't it? So why did she still feel guilty that she'd kept him waiting?

As they rode down a well-worn trail leading out of town toward the Bar-W, she was mesmerized by the scenery. Wildflowers dotted the vast landscape, while birds flitted through the pines and cedars, their music filling the silence. Although it was summer, snow still tipped the peaks of the mountains in the distance.

"It's so beautiful," she commented. "The air is so different out here. So … pure," she said, unable to find another word for the clean fresh smell.

"It is," he agreed. "I don't leave the ranch if I don't have to."

"I remember you hated even coming into town to go to school," she said. "You've never wanted to travel, have you?"

He shook his head. "No need. I have everything I want right here." He reached out and squeezed her hand, smiling at her. "Especially now."

Chloe's heart skipped a beat, and warmth filled her. Tamping down the unwanted emotions, she changed the subject. "How much farther do we have to go? I didn't realize your ranch was so far from town."

"Not much longer. I forgot you've never been to the Bar-W before."

Chloe chuckled. "I've never been anywhere before."

His brows arched. "Nowhere?"

"Not that I remember clearly. I went to Denver once when I was seven or eight years old, but all I remember are buildings. Lots and lots of buildings. I think that might have been when I decided that one day I would get out of Rocky Ridge and see the world."

He didn't respond. Whether it was because a squirrel suddenly darted in front of the wagon and one of the horses shied, or because of her words, she wasn't sure.

Once the horse calmed, she sat in silence, taking in her surroundings. It really was so peaceful, so spectacular without the constant noise in town, she could understand why Austin loved it so much. If she was willing to give up her dream of leaving, she might feel the same way.

As they reached the top of a small rise, Austin pulled on the reins and drew the wagon to a stop.

"Why are we stopping?" she asked.

"I wanted you to see the Bar-W from here."

She heard the pride in his voice as she gazed at the vista in front of her. Fields of thick emerald-green grass ended at the river, the water sparkling in the sunshine as it gurgled over rocks and a small waterfall.

In the distance, snow-tipped mountains rose to a clear blue sky.

Horses were contained in fenced pastures near

two large buildings she assumed were barns or stables, while cattle grazed as far as she could see.

A large log house stood near the barn, and several smaller buildings dotted the grounds nearby.

"I never tire of looking at this view," Austin said.

"I can see why," Chloe replied.

He shifted in his seat and faced her. "I hope you'll be happy here."

She could be. She could sense that. But her time here was temporary. She had to remember that.

"It's a mansion," Chloe said as Austin stopped the wagon in front of the house.

Austin laughed. "It's far from a mansion," he replied. "If you want to see mansions, go to New York City or England. Some of those houses would make this look like a cabin."

Guilt tugged at her conscience. She was eager to see England and New York City and every other sight she'd read about for years, but at the same time, the more time she spent with Austin, the more she realized how difficult it would be to follow through with Hattie's plan.

"It is big, though," Austin went on.

"Why did your parents build such a large house?" she asked.

Austin shrugged. "I don't know, but I think they hoped they'd have a lot of children to fill it."

"I'm surprised you don't get lost in all that space," she said with a chuckle. "I'm used to our small apartment above the diner."

Austin climbed out of the wagon and came around to help her out. Before he had a chance to lift her down, she stood up and stepped down. The wagon shifted, and she lost her balance, falling into his arms.

He staggered under the force of her body falling against him, but held her tightly against him until he regained his balance.

Her pulse raced, partly from the shock of falling but she suspected it had more to do with Austin's body pressing against hers.

Just then, the door opened and Jamie bounded down the stairs

Chloe planted her hands on Austin's chest and pushed him until he released her. Her face flamed at being caught in such an intimate position, but Jamie didn't seem to notice.

"Welcome to the Bar-W, Chloe."

"Thank you."

"I hope you don't mind me staying in the house for a bit longer," Jamie said. "It's been pretty busy around here, but I'll start building my own place as soon as I can, and I'll try to be out by Christmas."

Chloe had forgotten that Jamie also lived in the house with Austin. "Oh, no. Please don't leave on my account. There was only me and my papa for years, so it'll be nice to have more family. Please say you'll stay."

Jamie exchanged a glance with Austin and then turned back to Chloe. "If you're sure …"

"I am."

Jamie grinned. "In that case, I accept."

"I need to go and check on a sick calf," Jamie said, "so I'll leave you two alone. I'm sure you can manage without me." He slapped Austin on the back, planted his hat on his head and walked off.

"I hope you don't mind me telling Jamie to stay in the house with us," Chloe said.

"Not at all," Austin replied. "I didn't even think about it until yesterday when Jamie mentioned building his own place. I'm sure he'll want to be out on his own one of these days, but I'm really grateful that you're all right with him living with us, at least for now. "

"I am," she replied. She'd known Jamie almost as long as she'd known Austin, and they'd always been friendly. Their relationship was different from her friendship with Austin, though, she amended, and as they'd grown up, that hadn't changed.

Unlike her friendship with Austin. "He's your brother, and will always be welcome to stay with us as long as you want him to. Besides, the house is so big I'm sure we'll rarely see him, anyway."

Austin laughed. "That's true. There are times Jamie and I don't see each other for days."

"Does anyone else live here?"

"Just Dorcas, the housekeeper. She's been here as far back as I can remember. There is another woman comes in twice a week to help her now because she's not as young as she used to be, but she doesn't live here. Now come inside and let me show you around."

He led Chloe up the stairs to the porch and suddenly scooped her up in his arms.

She let out a squeal of alarm. "What are you doing?"

"Just carrying my bride over the threshold. I hear it's customary."

She giggled when he lowered her to the floor. "A warning would have been nice."

"I'm full of surprises," he said, laughing.

Chloe studied him for a few moments. His smile was infectious, and she soon found herself laughing with him. If she wasn't careful, she might start enjoying being married to him, and that would never do.

CHAPTER 8

*A*ustin opened one of six doors off a hallway on the second floor of the house. "And this is our bedroom," he said. He rested his hand on the small of her back and ushered her inside. "I hope you like it, but if not, go ahead and change whatever you want to. I don't really care what it looks like. I just sleep in here."

The room was beautiful just the way it was. A heavy oak dresser and wardrobe stood on one wall, a stuffed armchair and a small table with a lamp in another corner, its position perfect for gazing out the large window to the mountains in the distance.

The biggest bed Chloe had ever seen filled the opposite wall.

Four trunks were stacked against one wall. "I assume those are my trunks," Chloe said.

He nodded. "Dorcas offered to unpack for you, but I thought you'd prefer to do that yourself."

She also noticed an empty bookcase near the bed. "You have no books."

"It's for you. I know how important your travel books are to you," he said, following her gaze. "I knew you'd want them close by."

Her heart warmed. Austin really was so thoughtful.

"Thank you, but what about your books?"

"I don't have time to read much."

"That's a shame."

"Is there anything else I can do for you to make you more comfortable?" he asked.

She turned to face him. "I thought …" She hadn't planned on discussing their sleeping arrangements, but it seemed Austin expected them to still share a bed. "I expected to have my own room, especially since we're not … you know …"

"We're married," he reminded her. "You wanted folks to think we're in love, so how would it look if we slept in separate rooms?"

"No one would know."

He laughed then. "You're wrong. I trust Dorcas, but there are a lot of people who live on this ranch, and some of them even like to gossip. The truth would get out. If you want to take the chance, I'll move your trunks to another room."

"No," Chloe blurted out. She couldn't risk her father finding out her marriage was a sham. "You're right. I'll stay here."

"It won't be so bad," he assured her. "The bed is

big enough that it's not as if we'll even touch each other."

She was happy about that. At least, that's what she tried to tell herself. Yet deep inside, his words bothered her. It was what she wanted, wasn't it? A marriage in name only until such time that he'd want to send her away?

So why did she feel a little disheartened?

Once Austin and Jamie had finished discussing the schedule for the rest of the month and the repairs that needed to be done before the fall roundup, the conversation around the supper table that night turned more personal.

"I forgot to tell you," Jamie said as he stabbed his fork into a slice of roast beef on the china platter and put it on his plate. "Eddie Warner, the new foreman at the Flying-J rode by this afternoon with an invitation. George and Winnifred Jansen, the new owners, want to get to know the neighbors so they're throwing a party."

"Is that so? Have you met them yet?" Austin asked Jamie. He'd heard new people had bought out the ranch and stock from Abner Glass when he decided to go and live with his daughter in Texas.

"No, but I hear they have three daughters."

"Then I don't have to ask if you're planning on going."

Jamie shook his head and wiggled his eyebrows. "You don't. Just being neighborly, that's all."

"Sure. That's all." If there were unattached women around, Jamie would be close by. "You do realize now that I'm off the market, you're the prime target for all the mamas looking to get their daughters married off."

"They can try all they like," Jamie said. "I have no intention of settling down. Why would I restrict myself to one woman? That would be like having the same meal every day for the rest of my life."

"If it's the right meal ... or the right woman ... that's not such a bad thing," Austin put in, then turned his attention to Chloe. "Would you like to go to the party?"

Chloe nodded. "I would. Papa met the Jansens once when they came into the diner but I wasn't there."

"What were they like?" Jamie asked. "Did he say?"

"He liked them very much," she replied. "He told me they'd just returned from spending the winter in Europe and Great Britain. It'll be interesting to speak with them about their travels."

"Yeah," Austin murmured. He only hoped meeting them wouldn't make Chloe more unhappy than she already was.

After almost a week of doing nothing productive, Chloe was ready to scream. Even before she was old enough to really help her father in the diner, she'd had chores to do.

While it was relaxing not to have any responsibilities, the days dragged on and on. She began to look forward to evenings when she could retire to her room and sleep.

Thanks to Dorcas and Mildred, the woman who helped Dorcas a few days a week, she had nothing to do at all. It was bad enough that she was being treated like a fragile doll, but twice now, she'd been hustled out of the kitchen when she'd ventured into Dorcas's domain and offered to help.

Chloe wandered upstairs to her bedroom and closed the door behind her. She couldn't even take a dustmop to the room. Dorcas had already cleaned it, and there wasn't a speck of dust anywhere.

She had to find something to occupy her time.

Yet at the same time, the evenings were some of the most pleasant she'd ever spent. After supper, she and Austin usually retired to the main room where they'd talk or play checkers. Once in a while, Jamie joined them, but the other nights, they were alone.

Austin was kind and considerate, and he made her laugh. She'd forgotten how much she used to laugh when they spent afternoons together at the pond outside of town.

She never would have believed she could feel as if the ranch was home, but she did. In just a few days, it felt like she'd been here her whole life. That she belonged here. With Austin.

Her breath caught in her throat at the realization that her feelings for him were changing. She couldn't say why, because there was no particular incident that had affected her, but somehow, over the past few weeks since their "engagement", she'd begun to see him as a man, not as the boy who'd been her friend.

Perhaps that was why she was finding it so difficult now to put Hattie's plan into motion. She cared about Austin, perhaps more than she realized.

She wouldn't think about that now. She had to remember her dream, her goal for her life. Right now, though, her only goal was to find something to do.

She crossed to the window and gazed outside. Faint voices from one of the fenced corrals near the barn carried on the air. Men stood around watching as another man worked with a horse inside the enclosure.

Austin had been too busy since the wedding to show her around the ranch, but there was no reason she couldn't wander outside and take a closer look at the activity going on close by. Not that she'd want to get too close. Horses were huge beasts, and frankly, they terrified her.

But, she reasoned, if she planned to travel the world, she was sure she'd run into other situations that would frighten her. The sooner she learned to face her fears, the better.

She could start right now, and it would be reasonably safe to observe from a distance.

Her spirit renewed, she grabbed her bonnet and hurried outside.

Austin stood outside the corral, his arms leaning on the top rail, one of his booted feet resting on the bottom rail. His foreman, Curtis, stood beside him, watching the mare as it trotted back and forth inside the corral.

The mare shook her head and let out a soft whinny as if she was pleased that the men were there.

"She's come along real good, boss," Curtis said. "Jake had her out for a run earlier this morning and she's ready."

"Good, good," Austin replied absently. His attention was focused on Chloe crossing the yard and heading in his direction.

His heartbeat sped up the way it always did when he saw her. Desire speared him low inside, and his blood heated. He hadn't thought it was possible to love her more than he had before he married her. He'd been wrong. Being with her these past few days, breathing in her lavender scent, seeing her smile and feeling her skin against his as she slept had only intensified his feelings for her.

This was the first time she'd left the house since

she'd arrived and he hoped it was a sign she was interested in the goings-on around the ranch.

In a sudden gust of wind, her bonnet blew off her head. Luckily the ribbons around her neck prevented it from flying off into the breeze. She grabbed it and put it back on her head, tucking her hair inside as she approached him. She stopped a few yards back from the corral fence.

The mare wandered over to where the men were standing. Austin reached out and ran his hand down the horse's face.

"What are you doing?" Chloe asked.

He didn't answer, but asked a question of his own. "Do you like her? She's beautiful, isn't she?"

"Yes," Chloe replied hesitantly.

"Why don't you come closer?"

"It's all right," she said. "I'm fine here."

Austin straightened and came to stand in front of her. "Are you afraid of horses?"

"No!"

His brows lifted.

"Well, maybe a little ... okay, a lot ... terrified, if you must know."

He chuckled.

Chloe's lips thinned and her eyes narrowed. "Don't you laugh at me, Austin. I can't help it if I've never been around horses. It's just that they're so ... big."

"I'm sorry," he said. "I'm not laughing at your

fear, but there's no need to be afraid of horses, especially Bluebell. She's the perfect horse for you."

Chloe's eyes widened. "Me?"

"If you're going to live on a ranch, you should have your own horse."

Chloe's face paled, and he noticed she took even another step back.

"Oh … no …"

Austin took her hand. "Do you think I'd ever want you to do something that might hurt you?"

"Well … no …"

The horse hung its head over the top rail of the fence, gazing at Austin with its huge eyes. Austin reached out and ran his hand down its neck. "Bluebell likes human contact. Why don't you try it? Don't be afraid. She won't hurt you."

Chloe didn't move immediately, then she finally squared her shoulders and approached the fence. Bluebell turned her head toward Chloe, as if she was waiting for Chloe to pet her.

Hesitantly, Chloe reached up and gingerly touched Bluebell's forehead with two fingers. She drew her hand away, and immediately, Bluebell nudged her hand.

"She's telling you she likes you," Austin said.

Chloe's face lit up, and her eyes sparkled with pleasure. "She's so beautiful," she murmured.

"You don't know how to ride, do you?"

Chloe shook her head. "Living in town, I never

had any reason to learn. And any time I left town, we rented a buggy. I never had to get close to horses."

"You don't live in town now," he reminded her with a smile. "Living on a ranch, you should know how to ride. We're pretty busy this week, but I can teach you next week if you'd like to learn."

Chloe looked up at him. "Oh … I …." She took in a deep breath and let it out slowly. Then she nodded. "Okay."

"Good. The ranch is pretty big. There's so much I want to show you but we can't take a wagon or buggy."

Austin couldn't help feeling as if this was a step in the right direction. The more Chloe became involved in ranch life, the more chance there was that she might eventually be happy there.

CHAPTER 9

*L*anterns strung up on tree branches lit up the Flying-J's large yard. A wooden dance floor had been built, and musicians were busy tuning their instruments when Austin drew the wagon to a stop near other wagons, buckboards and horses tethered to a corral fence.

Chloe hadn't been to a party since … she couldn't really remember, but it had been a long time.

She'd been looking forward to this night ever since Jamie told them about it. She couldn't wait to talk to the Jansens and learn everything she could about their travels through Europe and Britain.

Austin had assumed her excitement was nothing more than eagerness to see her friends and enjoy herself. While that was true, Chloe hadn't pointed out that she had other reasons for her eagerness to get to the party early as well.

A group of children raced by, one turning back

and throwing a quick "sorry, ma'am" in Chloe's direction. She grinned.

"Food's over there." Jamie jerked his head in the direction of several tables nearby loaded down with food.

"I'm not surprised that's the first thing you'd look for," Austin teased.

Jamie shook his head. "Not the first thing," he replied. "I'll see you later," he added as he walked off in the direction of Sophia Costello and her father, newcomers to Rocky Ridge.

"Have I told you yet how pretty you look tonight?" Austin moved to stand closer to Chloe.

She flushed at the compliment. "Thank you." She was wearing one of her best dresses, pale pink with a white underskirt and white ruffles around the sleeves. She'd taken pains with her hair, too, pulling it back and arranging it in ringlets that fell to her shoulders.

"I see Rusty Standish over there," Austin said a few minutes later. "I do need to speak to him. It's business. Do you mind? I won't be long."

Chloe shook her head. "Not at all."

She stood for a few moments after Austin walked away, her gaze scanning the crowd. More and more people were arriving every minute, and she was surprised she hadn't caught sight of her father or Hattie yet.

"Mrs. Hayward?"

The voice behind Chloe startled her. She spun

around to find a woman she didn't recognize standing behind her. "Oh … yes …" She smiled.

The woman held out her hand. "I'm Winnifred Jansen," she said. "I'm so glad you could come."

Chloe shook her hand. "Thank you for inviting us, Mrs. Jansen."

"Please, it's Winnifred."

"Of course, and I'm Chloe. Welcome to Rocky Ridge, although I must admit I'm surprised you'd want to settle here."

Winnifred's brows arched. "Oh? Why is that?"

"Well," Chloe replied. "I heard that you and your husband have traveled the world. It's very quiet here and I'm sure it's not nearly as interesting as some of the places you've seen."

Winnifred chuckled. "It is much quieter, I agree, but now, it's what we're ready for. A quiet life. I've been lucky enough to see some of the most wondrous sights—"

"I'd so love to talk to you about your travels," Chloe gushed. "Did you go to Paris? Rome? Greece?"

"Yes," she replied with a laugh. "Among others. I loved them all. We threw coins into the Trevi Fountain and made a wish that we'll return some day. We strolled along the Champs-Élysées and saw the Parthenon in Athens. Sailed to Tahiti and Fiji … I could go on and on …"

"I'd love to hear all about it," Chloe said. "It's my dream to see the world."

Winnifred rested her hand on Chloe's arm. "Then

we'll make plans to have tea one day next week and I'll tell you everything."

"Wonderful." Excitement bubbled inside Chloe. Winnifred was the first person she'd ever met who had actually been to the places Chloe had only seen in photographs. She couldn't wait to hear about her adventures.

Winnifred waved to someone behind Chloe. "Unfortunately," she said, "right now I must see to our other guests."

"Oh … of course."

Chloe watched Winnifred walk away after she assured Chloe she'd send a message to the Bar-W with an invitation to tea.

The music was beginning, and once Winnifred disappeared into the crowd, Chloe turned her attention to the couples filling the dance area. She tapped her foot in time and hummed along with the lively tune as the dancers spun and twirled to the quadrille the musicians were playing.

It seemed everyone from Rocky Ridge and the surrounding ranches and farms had decided to come to the party. She wasn't surprised, though. People worked hard every day to make a future for themselves, so whenever they had the opportunity to get together with their neighbors and relax and enjoy themselves, they took advantage of it.

As she watched the dancers, she noticed Mrs. Worsley and Ann walking across the yard toward the dance area. It was unusual to see either of them at any town activities or celebrations. They usually kept to themselves and their own close circle of friends.

Chloe's lips quirked in a smile. Mrs. Worsley was likely looking for another match for Ann now that Austin wasn't available. Where was Austin anyway? she wondered.

Another quick look around and she found him—with Luisa Montello. Luisa was the most beautiful woman in town, with coal-black hair that curled around her shoulders, flashing dark eyes and voluptuous curves every man in town lusted after. She was gazing up at Austin, her hand resting on his arm, and he was laughing at something she was saying. Not just a slight chuckle, but a full-out belly laugh.

Chloe's stomach twisted. Her teeth clenched, and her hands fisted at her sides. Anger burned inside her. What was he doing? Had he forgotten he was a married man?

As for Luisa, she had a sudden urge to march over there and tear her luxurious hair out by the roots.

Mercy! She was jealous! But why? What was wrong with her? Why did she care what Austin did with another woman? It wasn't as if she was in love with him. She should be happy that he was enjoying himself, and if that enjoyment included another woman, she shouldn't have a problem with it.

Once she was gone, no doubt he'd marry again. She'd seen for herself over the years how women flocked around him, so it wouldn't be difficult for him to find a suitable wife.

She wanted him to be happy, didn't she? She cared about him. She always had, so if he could find a woman who'd make him happy, she should be glad. Then she could go on with her life the way she'd planned without any guilt, knowing she hadn't hurt him.

Perhaps he'd even decide that Luisa was the woman he wanted to spend his life with. And that should make Chloe happy. So why didn't it?

Austin and Luisa. The thought of the two of them together … Austin kissing Luisa … holding her … sharing his life with her …

She muttered a very unladylike word, then glanced guiltily around to be sure no one had heard her. Was did she feel so angry, and at the same time, so very sad.

The music began. Chloe closed her eyes momentarily as the strains of the familiar tune flowed through her.

"Care to dance?"

Austin's voice startled Chloe. She'd been lost in thought and hadn't seen him weaving his way through the other guests. "It's all right," she replied. "I know you don't dance."

"It's not that I don't like it exactly. I'm just not very good at it. I think I can manage a waltz though, so I probably won't embarrass you."

Chloe looked up at him, suddenly seeing him in a

different light. He was her husband, the man she'd vowed to spend her life with.

He was a good man. A kind man. A man who worked hard and treated her well. And a man who'd also made a huge sacrifice to help her father.

She could do worse than spend her life with Austin. She'd always liked him, and somehow, over the past few weeks, she'd grown to like him even more than she always had. But there was something more, something she couldn't quite explain to herself, something deeper, richer and more intense.

"Is it that hard to decide if you want to be seen on the dance floor with me?" His voice interrupted her thoughts.

She laughed. "Sorry, I was thinking about something else." That I like being with you and I miss you when you're gone, she could have added. "I'd love to dance with you."

He took her hand and as he led her to the dancing area, the sensations she'd often noticed snaking up her arms or through her body whenever he touched her filled her again. She made a mental note to talk to Hattie about it.

Austin's arm slid around her waist and he drew her closer, his hand splaying on her back. He began to move to the music, his steps a little awkward, but she managed to follow him around the floor.

All too soon, the music stopped. She smiled up at him. "You waltz much better than I expected," she said. "Who taught you?"

He leaned down and whispered. "Don't tell anybody, but it was Jamie."

"Jamie?" Her gaze slid to the other side of the floor where Jamie was waltzing with Cora Sweet, who was looking up at him with undisguised admiration.

"He told me it was a skill I needed to learn because ladies like to dance," Austin continued.

"That does sound like something he'd say," she commented. "Well, he was a good teacher."

Still holding her hand, he led her to a bench under one of the trees away from the guests milling around the dance floor and the tables holding the food. "We should do this more often," he said.

Chloe gave him an inquiring glance. "Do what?"

"Dance," he said, wiggling his brows. "I do like having you in my arms."

A slow heat built inside Chloe at his words. "You do?"

"I do. Very much."

Her heartbeat thundered in her ribs, and for a moment, she thought he was going to kiss her right then and there in front of everybody. She should be mortified at the thought of such a display in public, but instead, all she could think of was the touch of his lips on hers.

She forgot to breathe as their eyes met.

"There you are." Jamie came to stand beside them. "Chloe, come on. You're always my partner for this dance."

"What? Oh …"

"You go," Austin said with a smile. "I'll wait for you."

Jamie grabbed her hand. As she turned her back on Austin, she thought she heard him say something, but when she looked behind her, all she saw was him watching her.

"I'll always be here waiting for you," Austin muttered to himself as he watched Chloe walk away with his brother.

When she suddenly spun around and a frown marred her forehead, he thought she might have heard him, but she turned back and disappeared into the crowd of couples setting up for the dance.

He looked on as the music began and the four couples in the square began the dance. Jamie and Chloe spun, dipped and wove their way between the other dancers without missing a beat. He sighed, knowing he'd never be able to memorize the intricate steps they made look so easy.

Chloe's eyes were sparkling and she was smiling and laughing as Jamie swept her around the dance floor.

It was nice to see her smile and laugh. He'd tried to make her happy. He'd done everything he could to show her they could have a good marriage, but the truth of the matter was, nothing he'd done—or likely ever could do—would give her the life she wanted.

The life she'd dreamed about for as long as he'd known her.

She liked him. He knew that. But she didn't love him, and she didn't want to be married to him. He'd been a fool to think that by bribing her into a marriage that he could change her mind, that he could eventually make her love him.

He had to admire her for her sacrifice, though. Not many women—or men, for that matter, would have done what she'd done. She'd given up her future for someone else. It showed her love and loyalty for her father, and he was sure that if, one day, she had a husband she loved, she'd show him that same devotion.

She deserved to have a future she wanted, not one she'd been forced into. Guilt overwhelmed him.

He'd seen her smile earlier, too, when she'd been speaking with Winnifred Jansen. He hadn't been close enough to hear the conversation, but he could guess by the smile on her face what they were talking about - travel. Seeing the world outside the ranch, outside Rocky Ridge, outside Colorado.

He looked on as the dance continued. She was the woman he'd love until the day he died. Did he love her enough to make her happy even when his own happiness would be destroyed? For her to be happy, she needed her freedom, the one thing he'd taken away from her.

But did he love her enough to let her go?

CHAPTER 10

*A*ustin hurried out as soon as he'd finished his breakfast the next morning, leaving Chloe alone at the table. On the ride home from the party, he'd barely spoken to her, and he'd disappeared into his study as soon as they got back to the ranch. She'd been asleep when he'd finally come to bed.

He'd barely spoken to her during breakfast, and he'd muttered that he had a lot to do before he'd rushed out, without the quick kiss that had become a habit whenever he left the house.

She couldn't help wondering if he was angry with her. She should be happy if he was, but instead, for some reason it bothered her and made her miserable.

If he was annoyed with her, she wanted to know why.

Austin was working in one of the stalls at the rear of the barn when she went inside an hour later. He'd taken his shirt off and hung it over one of the stall rails and was shoveling straw into a wheelbarrow.

She stopped in the entrance, taking in his bare chest. She'd known he had muscles. She'd seen them when he undressed for bed every night, but something about the way they moved in the beam of sunlight streaming through a small window in the back wall drew her attention more than she wanted them to.

He hadn't heard her come in, so she stood stock-still, watching the play of those muscles in his back as he moved, taking in the breadth of his shoulders and the way his chest tapered to his waist.

Her throat dried up and a faint shivery trembling washed over her as an achy sensation filled her. She didn't understand it, but this wasn't the time to stop and analyze it.

He looked in her direction and, seeing her there, lowered the shovel and rested it against the stall gate. "Going for a ride?"

"No." Since that first day at the corral, he'd given her riding lessons every day. At first, she'd been terrified to even sit on Bluebell's back, but with his encouragement, she'd learned quickly.

The day before, Curtis had saddled Bluebell and she'd gone for her first ride alone. She hadn't gone far, but the freedom she'd felt with the power of the horse beneath her and the wind in her hair was unlike anything she'd ever known.

"You need something then?"

She took in a calming breath and crossed the dirt

floor to face him. "Yes, I do. I need to know what's wrong."

He didn't answer immediately, which assured her the change in him wasn't her imagination. "I just have a lot on my mind, that's all."

"Is it something I've done?" she asked.

"No." He picked up the shovel.

"Austin! Talk to me! We were always able to talk to each other. That was one of the things I loved about our friendship. Why can't you talk to me now?"

He stood with the shovel, the blade resting on the ground, his arm draped over the handle. "I will, once I straighten some things out in my mind." He cut her a faint smile. "I promise."

She wasn't satisfied with his answer, but she knew he wouldn't change his mind. He'd talk to her when he was ready, not before. She only hoped it wouldn't take long.

"I can't spare the time for you to spend the afternoon visiting with everyone," Austin told Chloe a few days later when he drew the wagon to a stop in front of the mercantile in Rocky Ridge.

"I understand," Chloe replied. "I hate to take you away from the ranch, and once I learn how to drive the wagon, you won't have to bring me into town."

He didn't respond to her comment about driving the wagon, just as he'd made excuses for the past few days why he couldn't give her more riding lessons.

Something wasn't right. Ever since the party, he'd been quieter than normal, and he still hadn't told her what was bothering him.

Was he annoyed she'd danced with Jamie? Had she done something else to upset him?

She'd tried to talk to him again the day before, and he'd assured her everything was fine, but the closed expression in his eyes told her otherwise. Still, she had no choice but to accept what he said and hope that one day, he'd be willing to talk.

"How long will your business take at the bank?" she asked as she climbed out of the wagon.

He shrugged. "Likely an hour or so."

"I'll only be a few minutes in the mercantile so I'll have time for a short visit with my father. Since he didn't go the party at the Jansen ranch, I've missed him. I'm worried he might be sick or hurt."

"Jamie was in the diner a couple days ago and he was fine. He was likely too busy to go to the party, that's all."

"You didn't mention it—"

He shrugged. "Didn't think of it. Sorry."

"Well, I'm glad he's not ill, and I'm anxious to see how he's doing now that the diner is open again."

"I'll pick you up there when I'm finished then."

He smiled, but it didn't reach his eyes. Something was clearly upsetting him.

"That's fine," she replied. "I'll be ready to leave whenever you are."

As Austin drove away, she went up the steps to the mercantile. She was choosing a length of fabric for a new skirt a few minutes later when Hattie rushed up and threw her arms around her. "Chloe! It's so good to see you! It's been forever!"

Chloe returned Hattie's hug, then released her and took a step back. "It does seem like a long time." She held a piece of fabric up to the light coming through the window.

"What are you doing in town? How long are you staying? Can you come to the house for a visit?"

"I'm sorry, I can't today. I want to go and see my father."

The smile on Hattie's face faded, and she looked away, focusing on a piece of ribbon on the shelf above the fabric display.

"What is it, Hattie? Has something happened to my father?"

"No," Hattie assured her. "He's fine. It's just … I don't know if I should even mention it, but—"

"But what?"

"Well, I saw him go into the saloon yesterday."

Chloe's stomach dropped. She'd hoped and prayed this time would be different, that her father would finally have slayed the demons that drove him to gamble.

"I'm so sorry, Chloe," Hattie went on. "I wasn't going to tell you, but I thought you should know."

Chloe nodded. "I'm glad you told me. Now if you'll excuse me, I'm going to go to the diner and find out what's going on."

After another hug and a quick goodbye, Chloe paid for her purchases and left the mercantile.

Chloe marched down the boardwalk toward the diner. Anger and frustration warred with sadness and hurt inside her. Thoughts swirled in her brain.

She was surprised to see the Closed sign on the door, although this time of day wasn't usually busy. It was still early, and the diner wouldn't fill up for another hour or so.

Using her key, she let herself in and crossed to the stairs leading to the apartment upstairs. "Papa? Are you here?" she called out.

Only silence met her ears.

The rooms were tidy, which surprised her. She'd wondered how his housekeeping skills would be when she wasn't there to clean for him. It seemed she wasn't needed after all.

There was no sign of her father, so she went back downstairs and left, locking the door behind her. She paused on the boardwalk, her gaze scanning the street.

Slowly, she made her way down the street toward the bank, where Austin had said he'd be. As she passed the saloon, a familiar voice reached her ears. Her father's voice.

Sadness overwhelmed her. She'd been so sure he wouldn't break his promise to her this time. She'd been wrong.

She should keep going, pretend she didn't know he'd fallen into his old habits again. Wash her hands of him and his problem.

She took a few steps past the entrance, then stopped. She couldn't do it. She couldn't forsake him. He was her father, and she loved him. She couldn't turn her back on him no matter what he'd done.

Spinning around, she pushed on the batwing doors with the heels of her hands and stormed into the saloon. And stopped dead in her tracks.

Her father was sitting at one of the round tables that dotted the room, but instead of cards in his hand, he was holding a pencil and paper. Beside both men were mugs of coffee.

Herman Barron, the saloon owner, sat facing him. Both men looked up as the doors swung behind her.

"Chloe!" Elvin bounded out of the chair and hurried toward her, reaching out and pulling her into his beefy arms.

The scent of his shaving soap filled her nose, and for a moment, she had that same sensation of love and comfort she'd always felt as a little girl wrapped in her papa's embrace.

He released her, holding her at arm's length. "You look well," he said. "What brings you to town?"

"Austin had business," she replied, trying to look behind him to see what the papers were on the table. "I went to the diner but it wasn't open."

Elvin shook his head. "Had business of my own to take care of, and I'm waiting on the next beef shipment to come. It's late again, so right now all I can serve people is chicken and pork. I'll be opening up again at noon."

She couldn't hold her tongue any longer. It didn't look like he was gambling again, but what other possible reason could he have for being in a saloon? "What's happening here?"

Elvin grinned and wrapped an arm around her shoulders, drawing her toward the table. He held a chair out for her to sit down. She perched on the edge and set her reticule on the table beside her. "I'm glad you happened to be in town today. I want your opinion since you're the owner of the diner now."

"Pa, you own the diner—"

"Don't go arguing with me, girl," he insisted. "Just look at this." With a grin, he slid a piece of paper toward her.

She looked down, her eyes taking in the scrawling writing on the page. It was a list—wishes she'd made in the diner, and prices listed beside it. "What is this?"

Herman's booming voice interrupted. "Your pa and I have been talking for a while now, and I think we've finally worked out a deal. I have three rooms upstairs for rent. I want to supply meals to the boarders if they want them. I don't have the room or the inclination to cook, so your pa has agreed to supply whatever meals I need. At a discount from his regular diner prices, of course," he added with a laugh.

Chloe had to force herself not to grin too widely. It seemed her suspicions—and her fears—were unfounded.

"What do you think, poppet?" Elvin asked her. "Do you think it's fair?"

She studied the numbers, then nodded. "I do," she said.

"Good," Elvin said, standing up and holding out his hand. "Then it's settled, Herman. We have a deal."

Herman took it and the men shook hands. "Where's Austin?"

"He had some business at the bank, then he's coming to the diner to take me back to the ranch."

"Then we'd better get back," Elvin said, ushering her toward the door. "We don't want to keep him waiting." Turning to Herman, he raised his hand in a small wave.

They strolled quietly down the boardwalk toward the diner. Austin was slowing the wagon in front of the diner as they approached.

Austin climbed out of the wagon and shook Elvin's hand. Chloe had worried there might be some awkwardness between the two men as a result of that fateful poker game, but it seemed her concerns were unwarranted.

"We'd better get moving, Chloe," Austin said a few minutes later after Elvin told him the latest news.

"Of course," she replied, then rose on her tiptoes to kiss her father's cheek. "Before I go, Papa, tell me. How are you really?"

She knew he was well aware of what she was asking. He cupped her head in his hands and kissed her forehead. "I'm fine. Really fine," he added as if to reassure her. "What happened taught me a hard lesson. I have a second chance, and even though it's tempting sometimes just to stop into the saloon in the evenings, I know I can't. Now you go home and don't you worry about me."

Chloe let Austin help her into the wagon, feeling more relaxed than she had since the day Austin proposed. Now that she was more confident in her father's ability to stay away from the poker table, the only thing on her mind was Austin.

CHAPTER 11

he heavy rains that had been falling for two solid days had finally stopped that morning, and a watery sun peeked through the wispy clouds overhead.

Chloe took off her bonnet and set it on top of her reticule on the dresser and dropped to the side of the bed.

That morning, one of the hands from the Flying-J had brought a note from Winnifred Jansen inviting her to tea. It had been hard to contain her excitement. She'd never met anyone who'd traveled as much as the Jansens and she couldn't wait to hear about the places she'd dreamed of and the sights she'd always wanted to see.

She'd been so looking forward to spending some time with Winnifred, and even though driving the wagon was much harder than the buckboard, she'd managed to drive the wagon alone to the Flying-J after lunch.

She'd enjoyed listening to her tales of Winnifred's adventures traveling through Europe and the South Pacific, yet all during the visit she'd actually found herself anxious to get back to the Bar-W.

It was all so very strange.

She let her gaze drift to the bookcase and peruse some of the titles on the shelves—*Palmetto Leaves*, by Harriet Beecher Stowe, *Wild Wales*, by George Borrow, and one of her favorites, *Pictures from Italy*, by Charles Dickens.

She plucked out a copy of Isabella Bird's *The Hawaiian Archipelago* and leafed through the pages. She'd always planned that one day, she'd see it for herself. Now, for some reason she didn't understand, she found herself thinking more about the fall roundup Austin had told her about, Thanksgiving, and Christmas gifts for the ranch hands …

The door opened and Austin walked in. "You're back," he said, tossing his hat on the bed. "How was your visit?"

"Fine," she said.

"Just fine? You were so excited about the invitation."

She couldn't explain to Austin what she didn't understand herself. She had been so eager to visit with Winnifred, to hear about her travels, but even as her new friend had been telling her about sailing between the Hawaiian Islands and eating roast pig the natives cooked in a pit, she'd been wondering what was going on back at the ranch. One of the mares was about to foal, and another had hurt her hoof a few days before. She hadn't had a chance to check on them before she left.

"I was excited," she said. She closed the book and slid it back into the empty space on the shelf. "It's strange how life just doesn't turn out the way you expect it to, isn't it?"

"It is," he agreed.

Something in his expression bothered her, although she couldn't put a finger on it. He still hadn't told her what was preying on his mind, but the way he was studying her, his gaze intense, frightened her.

Chloe was snipping dead blooms off the honeysuckle that grew along the side of the house the next afternoon. Movement out of the corner of her eye caught her attention. Austin was crossing the yard toward her. She smiled up at him when he reached her. "Are you finished all your chores?" she asked. "Supper won't be ready for another hour."

"We need to talk."

The expression on her face told her something was very wrong. Her smile evaporated and her heartbeat stuttered. "What is it? Has something happened to my father?"

"No," he assured her. "As far as I know, your pa is

fine." He took the shears out of her hand and dropped them into the basket. "Come and sit beside me on the porch."

He held onto her hand and led her up the stairs. Once she was sitting in one of the rocking chairs, he sat in the other, still holding her hand.

Something must be terribly wrong, she thought. She'd never known Austin to be at a loss for words. She waited, wondering how long it would take him to tell her what was on his mind. Finally, he spoke.

"I made a mistake. A big mistake."

"What kind of mistake?" she asked. "Whatever it is, we can make it right."

He tried to smile, but it didn't reach his eyes. Those eyes, eyes that usually twinkled with good humor, were … sad. "That's what I'm trying to do."

He took off his hat and raked his fingers through his hair. "This isn't working," he said.

Her brow furrowed. "What's not working?"

"This. Us. Our marriage."

Chloe couldn't believe what she was hearing. She sucked in a gasp, and she felt her mouth form an "O". Her heart hammered against her ribs. "I see," she murmured a few moments later.

"I'm so sorry I did this to you," he went on. "I had no right to force you into a marriage you didn't want."

"Austin—"

His voice cracked with emotion. "And because I need to make things right, I'm letting you go. I thought I could be satisfied with your friendship, that it would be enough. But it isn't. I care about you enough that I want you to be happy, so I'm going to find out how to get the marriage annulled as soon as I can. That way you can have the life you want."

Before she had time for his announcement to even sink in, he got up and walked away.

Chloe sniffled back her tears and dabbed at her eyes with a lace handkerchief. "He didn't come back last night," she told Hattie.

The two women were sitting at Hattie's kitchen table the next morning, mugs of steaming coffee and fresh-from-the-oven cinnamon rolls in front of them.

She could have gone to the diner, but right now, she needed a woman's ear, a woman's sympathy. Besides, she was afraid of her father's reaction once she told him what had happened. He was likely to go out to the ranch and beat Austin to a pulp.

She'd sat on the porch in stunned shock for quite some time after Austin walked away, her brain trying to process what he'd told her.

He cared about her, but he wanted to escape their marriage. It made no sense.

Eventually, she'd gone inside, told Dorcas she wasn't feeling well and didn't want supper, and she'd gone to their room to start packing.

She'd expected him to come in to sleep, but as the

hours went by, she realized he wasn't coming. She'd lain awake the entire night, feeling as if she'd been trampled by a dozen horses and left to die.

Shortly after dawn, she'd asked Curtis saddle Bluebell. She'd left a short note for Austin picked up her carpetbag, and she'd ridden away from the ranch. She'd packed her trunks and in the note, she'd asked Austin to please have someone bring them to town.

"I don't understand why you're so upset," Hattie said between licking icing off her fingers. "You'll be free again and your father will have the diner. It's all working out the way we planned."

"I know … it's what I wanted …"

As the words left her mouth, her heart constricted. It was what she wanted, wasn't it?

Well … yes, she still wanted to travel, but now, whenever she dreamed about the sights she'd see, somehow Austin was beside her, sharing them with her.

"You've fallen in love with him, haven't you?" Hattie's voice interrupted her thoughts.

She nodded. "I … have … I do … I love him." The weeks they'd spent together had changed her, and her feelings for him had grown from friendship to love. A love that consumed her and made it impossible to imagine life without him.

She wanted to spend her life with Austin, to be a real wife, to raise a family with him on the Bar-W.

"Then go back to him and tell him," Hattie said. "Refuse to get an annulment. You know there's a way to do that, and I don't know of any man who would refuse to bed a woman."

"It's too late …"

"It's only too late if you don't try."

Was Hattie right? Should she have fought for her marriage? She didn't know. After all, she hadn't even realized she'd fallen in love with Austin until just a few minutes ago.

The question was, what was she going to do about it? Hattie had told her to go to Austin and tell him how she felt, but she wasn't sure she had the courage.

If she didn't tell him, though, he'd have the marriage annulled and move on with his life. Without her.

She'd always believed she was brave enough to travel the world alone, facing the unknown without any help from anyone. There was even a chance that in some foreign land, she could be risking her life. She'd always been prepared to do just that.

But was she brave enough to confess to Austin and risk her heart?

"What was I saying?" Jamie asked Austin that night. The two men were in the small room off the kitchen they used as an office.

Austin looked across the desk at his brother. "What?"

"You have no idea what I said about selling off a

hundred head to Booker Abrahams over in Cedar Valley, do you?"

Austin shook his head. He hadn't been paying any attention to business. Instead, he'd been wrapped up in his own misery.

He'd given Chloe what she wanted - her freedom. His chest squeezed like it was caught in a blacksmith's vice and he could barely draw a breath, but it had been the right thing to do.

He'd forced her into this marriage, and he'd righted the wrong he'd done her.

"Sorry," he muttered.

"Whatever's going on in your head—and I'd wager it has something to do with you and Chloe, fix it."

Austin hadn't told Jamie that his marriage was over. He'd explained Chloe's absence at supper by telling him she was spending the night in town to help Hattie with some preserves she was making. "It's not that simple," Austin pointed out.

"It is." Jamie collected the papers they'd been going over and arranged them in a neat stack. "You really don't know much about women, do you?"

"Sure I do—"

Jamie's brows lifted. "How many women have you courted?"

Austin didn't answer. He didn't have to. Jamie knew exactly how many women he'd had his heart set on. One. Chloe. He'd never courted her, but he'd never had any interest in courting any other woman either.

"That's what I thought," Jamie went on. "If you love Chloe, and I know you do, give her what she wants."

Maybe it was time to tell Jamie what he'd done. "That's what I did. I gave her back her freedom so she can go see the world like she's always dreamed of."

Jamie shook his head. "For a fella who's usually pretty smart, you're pretty stupid sometimes."

Austin's temper rose. "Jamie, you better watch your tongue. Brother or not—"

"You love her," Jamie went on, "and if I know anything at all about women, and I've known Chloe as long as you have, she loves you, too."

What was Jamie talking about? Before he had a chance to ask, Jamie continued.

"She does. She might not even know it yet, but I can see it plain as day. She doesn't want her freedom, but she does want to see outside this town. Should be pretty easy to figure out how to make her happy, even for a dolt like you."

Jamie was smiling, which was the only reason Austin didn't get up and slug him for the insult.

"Your mind isn't on business, so I'm going to turn in. Fix your marriage before you ruin everything."

Jamie walked out, leaving Austin to mull over his brother's words of advice. How was he supposed to fix it? Chloe didn't love him. He'd always known that, but he'd thought he loved her enough for both of them.

Something niggled at him. A thought that flitted through his brain, a wisp of an idea how he could still make her happy without giving her up. They could both have what they wanted.

He was still sitting at his desk when the first rays of sunshine brightened the office the next morning. At some point during the night, a plan had begun to form in his mind, and as soon as he could get to town, he'd start making it happen.

CHAPTER 12

*I*t was three days later when a knock came to Hattie's door. Hattie opened it and seeing Austin standing on the porch, hat in hand, scowled and slammed it shut.

Austin knocked again. And again. "Open the door and let me talk to Chloe."

"She's not here."

"Elvin told me she's here." Austin's eyes narrowed and his lips drew into a thin line.

"She doesn't want to see you."

"I'm not going away until I talk to her," he insisted.

Footsteps sounded on the porch, then silence.

Hattie closed the door and turned to Chloe, who was standing at the bottom of the staircase, out of Austin's sight. "What do you want me to do?"

Chloe crossed to the window and hooked the edge of the curtain back with one finger. She peeked around to see Austin sitting in the rocker on the porch, one leg crossed over the other, his hat hanging on his bent knee.

Her chest tightened, the lump in her throat threatening to choke her, and tears burning her eyes. She didn't want to see him, to know she'd lost him because of something that wasn't even important to her anymore.

But it looked like he was prepared for a long stay, if necessary, and the only way to get rid of him would be to face him. "Might as well let him in," she told Hattie.

She tucked a few stray strands of hair into the loose knot at her nape and smoothed down the apron she'd put on to help prepare lunch.

Hattie opened the door and Austin bounded up. The chair rocked violently and for a moment, it seemed as if it would tip, until he grabbed the back and steadied it.

He came inside, hat in hand. "Morning, Chloe," he said. He took a step toward her.

She backed away, muttering a greeting.

"I'll leave you two alone," Hattie put in, grabbing her bonnet from a hat stand near the door. "I have some weeding to do," she added as she hurried out, closing the door behind her.

"What do you want, Austin?" Chloe said finally when it appeared he was going to just stand there looking at her.

"I want you to come with me."

"Come with you where? And why would I do that?"

"So we can talk."

"I think you've said more than enough," she snapped. "Did you arrange the annulment?"

He shook his head. "Please come with me."

"I'm not dressed to go out," she pointed out.

He studied her, his gaze sliding from her head to her feet. "You're perfect."

She shouldn't go anywhere with him, but it seemed her mouth had other ideas. "I don't see the point."

"I'm hoping you will once we're there."

"Where are you taking me?"

He smiled, that smile that always melted her heart and heated her insides. "It's a surprise. You know you always liked surprises."

She did, and he knew it, but some surprises were devastating, as she'd found out. "Very well."

After telling Hattie she was going out for a while, she climbed into the wagon and Austin drove them out of town. A half hour later, he stopped the wagon near the pond where they'd swum and fished when they were children.

It hadn't changed much. Frogs croaked and bees buzzed and flitted among the wildflowers dotting the grass surrounding the pond. The rope Austin had tied to an outstretched tree branch still hung above the water.

"Why are we were?" she asked.

He helped her out of the wagon, then reached under a blanket draped in the wagon bed to produce a picnic basket.

"What's this?"

"It's a picnic basket," he said.

"I can see that, but why—"

He grinned. "Because we're going to have a picnic."

He folded the blanket and hung it over his arm and picked up the basket. Then he grabbed her hand and gently pulled her toward a willow tree near the bank of the pond.

"Austin—"

"Just wait."

She sighed.

In the shade of the willow, he put the basket on the grass and held two corners of the blanket out to her. She took them and helped him spread it on the grass.

"I'm not in the mood for a picnic," she ground out.

"I'm hoping you'll change your mind when you see what's inside."

She was confused, but she had to admit she was intrigued. What was he up to?

"Sit down," he said.

She did as he asked. "Now what?"

"We're going to eat," he said. "Open the basket."

Chloe let out a huff of frustration. "I don't know why you brought me all the way out here when you said everything you needed to say the other day. You made it very clear you don't want to be married to me —" Her eyes caught sight of an envelope lying on top of a loaf of fresh bread. "What's this?"

"Open it."

Gingerly, she slipped her finger beneath the flap of the envelope and tore it open, then reached inside and took out two small rectangular pieces of thick paper.

For a few moments, her brain refused to register what she was looking at. Then the words "RAIL TICKET" sank into her brain, and she saw her name printed on one of the tickets, Austin's on the other. The destination was New York City.

The envelope also held another piece of paper. She plucked it out and unfolded it. Her eyes skimmed the printing on the page—dates, times, places.

She looked up at him. A grin split his face and his eyes shone. She held up the two train tickets in one hand and the piece of paper in the other. "I don't understand—"

"The train tickets will get us to New York City. The list is our itinerary of where we'll go after New York. It's not all finalized yet, but I couldn't wait to give it to you."

Chloe was speechless, likely for the first time in her life. She gazed at the names on the paper—Paris, London, Athens …

"How did you do this?"

"Getting train tickets to New York wasn't difficult,

and I have somebody in New York working on getting the steamship tickets, arranging hotels, etc."

"I ... I don't know what to say."

"Say you'll go with me," he said.

"But why? You don't like to travel."

"It's not that I wouldn't enjoy seeing the rest of the world, but I'm content to stay on the ranch, too. Because you married me, you had to give up your dream, and much as I wanted you to be happy, I knew you weren't. I didn't want to be responsible for that, so I decided to let you go."

"I already know all that."

He took a jar of lemonade and two glasses out of the picnic basket and poured them both a drink. He took a long drink of his, then went on.

"After you left the ranch, I realized I should have told you the truth about why I forced you to marry me." He looked down at her.

"You did tell me why you wanted to marry me," she said.

He shook his head. "That was the truth, but it wasn't the *whole* truth. I've spent the past few days trying to find the right words ..."

She reached up and rested her hand on his face. "Austin, we've always been able to tell each other anything. They don't have to be the *right* words. Any words will do. Just say what you want to say."

"You're right, as usual. We've always been able to be honest. There's one thing I wasn't honest about, though, and even though I'm willing to give you your life back if you still want it when I'm done, I aim to tell you the truth about the whole thing before I do."

"All right."

He raked his hand through his hair. "I'm sorry I bribed you into a situation you didn't want," he began. "I feel awful about it, but I had good reasons."

"I know that, and I understand—"

He shook his head. "I don't think you do. You see, I could have come up with some other way to make your father take the diner back, but asking you to marry me was much better. Because ..."

"Because what?"

"Because I wanted to marry you."

"I know that. You explained why when you asked me."

He let out a laugh. "I did, didn't I? It was true, but escaping the clutches of the single ladies in town wasn't the only reason I wanted to marry you."

Her brows arched. "What other reason could there be?"

He looked away, seemed to study the landscape for a long moment. Then he turned back to face her. She noticed he took in a deep breath before he spoke again.

"Because I love you," he murmured.

"What?"

"I love you," he repeated. "I've loved you for years, but you never saw me as more than a friend. Then, after we danced that night at your birthday party, it seemed we weren't even really friends anymore."

How was it possible that he loved her and she hadn't had any idea? "We are friends …" Now that she really thought about it, she had avoided him after the party, because something inside her had changed that night. She'd been uncomfortable with the way he made her feel, and she didn't understand why. It was easier to avoid him than to examine her feelings. Now, looking back, she realized what those feelings were. She was starting to fall in love with him even then, but she was so innocent and naïve, she hadn't realized it.

"I've missed you." He lowered his gaze and reached for her hand. "I want you to stay married to me, but I want you to be happy."

"Austin, I—""

"I don't want to end our marriage, but since you don't love me—"

She reached up and placed her finger on his lips to prevent him saying more. "I do."

His eyes widened, and he shifted her finger away from his mouth. "What did you say?"

"I love you, too," she said, her heart overflowing with love for this man who was willing to sacrifice his own happiness for hers. "I didn't know it until I thought I'd lost you."

"You do?"

Tears filled Chloe's eyes, but they were tears of happiness. "I have a secret of my own that I'm going to confess and hope you don't hate me."

"I could never hate you."

"When you proposed, Hattie and I came up with a plan to make you so unhappy being married to me that you'd want an annulment or a divorce. I wanted to follow through with it, but I couldn't."

"Why not?"

"Because … because as we grew closer, I discovered I didn't want our marriage to be over. When you sent me away, I realized I could go and see all the sights I'd dreamed about, but they didn't have any appeal. I wanted to be with you, not half way around the world. Alone. So if you still want me, you have me. For now and always."

Austin wrapped his arms around her and kissed her thoroughly. When they parted, her breathing was ragged. "I have one more plan," she said. "I want to be a real wife to you here on the Bar-W. I want to raise a family with you here, a family who'll take over the ranch one day. I want to grow old with you here, to sit on the porch and look out at the mountains and be content with the life we've had."

"I like your plan," he said, "and right now, I especially like the idea of filling the house with children."

She grinned and snuggled into the circle of his arms. "But first things first."

She gazed up at him. "What?"

He picked up the train tickets and waved them in front of her. "First, we need a honeymoon."

EPILOGUE

hree months later

Hand in hand, Chloe and Austin strolled across the courtyard outside Notre Dame Cathedral in Paris, France.

"It's spectacular, isn't it?" Chloe commented.

Austin nodded. "It is. We only have another day here in Paris, so do you want to spend it here or see something else?"

"We've seen so much," she began. "This trip has been more than I ever dreamed of, especially because you're with me."

"This is only the beginning," he reminded her. "We still haven't seen Rome, or Greece or—"

She raised herself onto her tiptoes and silenced him with a kiss. When she drew back, she smiled at him, her heart filled with more love than she could imagine. "I can't thank you enough for this, and for offering to show me more of the world we live in, but for now, I've had all the travel I want."

"You have?"

She nodded. "I've enjoyed every minute of this adventure, but right now there's something else I want more than seeing the Coliseum or the Parthenon."

"What's that? You know if it's at all possible, I'll give you anything you want."

"You can give me this," she assured him.

His brow furrowed. "What is it?"

"I miss Colorado. I miss Rocky Ridge, and I miss the Bar-W." She smiled at him, took his hand. "I want to go home."

"Home? Really?"

"Home," she repeated, "where we belong."

Where she'd belong forever.

ABOUT THE AUTHOR

Although she grew up far from the American west she writes about, Margery Scott has always been interested in stories about the men and women who settled the untamed land west of the Mississippi.

A transplanted Scot, Margery now lives in Canada with her husband. When she's not writing or traveling in search of the perfect setting for her next novel, you can usually find her wielding a pair of knitting needles or a pool cue.

Website: www.margeryscott.com
Email: margery@margeryscott.com
Newsletter: www.margeryscott.com/newsletter
VIP Facebook reader group: www.facebook.com/groups/margeryscott